VINNIE PINCHEY

VINNIE PINCHEY

BY

DANA PRIDE

Everlasting Publishing
Yakima, Washington
USA

Vinnie Pinchey

by
Dana Pride

ISBN-13: 978-0-9983858-1-5

First Edition
Everlasting Publishing
P.O. Box 1061
Yakima, WA 98907
USA

Dedicated to my husband, Rev. Willie F. Pride, Jr., for your support and love throughout this project. Also, I thank God for the dream that started it all.

In these days of abundance and luxury in our society, people have advantages and opportunities to live almost any way we want to live. Our desires and our choices shape our lives. In the days of Vinnie Pinchey, each person is encouraged to do what he wants to do, all the time, in the name of free choice. How does one person's free choice affect others? Can we really do whatever we want and still enjoy freedom?

VINNIE PINCHEY

VINNIE PINCHEY

The first time I ever heard about Vinnie Pinchey, I was in the girls' locker room at a public swimming pool. I had just finished swimming a few laps and was feeling a tad guilty, for two reasons: one, I felt that I should have stayed in the pool longer, for I love to swim and crave that kind of exercise; and two, I was already late for my appointment and didn't want to keep my family waiting any longer. So, I was toweling off the water as I walked through the nearly empty locker room, attempting to put my clothes on over my wet swimsuit as I walked, in order to save time.

As I was passing the low lockers in the middle of the room, I came upon a young girl of about ten or eleven years old, who was crying desperately while another girl, a bit older, most likely her sister, by their similar features and statures, was standing nearby watching her. Even in my hurry, I was drawn to help the poor girl, if I could possibly do anything for her. It would be fruitless to ask her anything, as she was wailing so loudly with her eyes smashed into slits, she was obviously oblivious to my presence; so, I paused in my haste and asked the other girl.

"What is the matter with her?"

"She's upset because she can't have her party be Vinnie Pinchey," the older sister said with a little shrug of her shoulders.

"What's Vinnie Pinchey?" I asked, my mind flying in a hundred directions of possibilities: was it a video game or a theme or a food or was it merely a phrase, such as 'cool,' or 'smashing,' as they used back in the day.

The younger sister continued to cry real tears as her shoulders shuddered, as if she were being tortured, while the older sister gave me a look that said I was too old to possibly understand, since I was so far removed from reality that I didn't know what Vinnie Pinchey was. Her glare replaced any kind of reply she may have given me.

"It's okay, I'll look it up on Google," I said, then immediately regretted that I had even responded, since, to her, Google was as ancient as a dial telephone: it had ceased to exist in her world, replaced by Siri, or whatever had already replaced the smart-aleck phone app.

I gave one more look at the younger sister, still in full-wail, and snapped my sundress over my swim suit as I slipped on my sandals, then made my way to the door. How could I – or anyone else – have known then that Vinnie Pinchey would be the first snowflake of the avalanche that destroyed the society of our entire country?

THE PLANNING OF VINNIE PINCHEY

Seven men sat behind closed doors in the 57th floor corner office in downtown Los Angeles, eager to hear the latest billion-dollar idea from Alan Jellitan. All eyes were on this man who sat at the head of the enormous glass table as he looked from one man to the next, grinning smugly.

"Gentlemen," he began, then he paused to light a cigarette. He knew he should quit smoking, but this was not the time. Big money was in this room, and his own genius mind was about to transform that huge amount into a landslide of funds - legally - for everyone at this table. He inhaled deeply as he prepared to give his pitch.

"We are about to embark on a journey to the golden land of financial success beyond any of our wildest dreams. The plans we have will create a global commerce shift as everyone in the entire world will be contributing to our financial success. I know you have been waiting for it, and here is our base product."

Alan Jellitan made a huge production of crushing out his cigarette in an ashtray and pulling a box from beneath his chair.

"What is it, a pair of shoes?" Thomas "Snarky" Snellburger asked, raising his eyebrow. "Just do it already."

"It is definitely not a pair of shoes," Alan announced loudly. He removed the lid and pulled an object from the box.

"Are you crazy?" Kenneth Shmatz said, thumping his hand on the table. "That is a doll."

The men exploded in laughter, shouting and jeering as Alan took the doll and gently stroked its hair.

"Jellitan, you have gone off your rocker," John Smattering said with a snort. "I am officially announcing that you are wasting our time. That is a doll!"

"It IS a doll, yes, but it is so much more than simply a doll. I am telling you here and now, and you can mark my words, this doll is the beginning of a movement!" Alan Jellitan announced proudly. "This is Vinnie Pinchey!"

The room was instantly silent, all eyes glued to the doll. The atmosphere turned solemn in an instant, as dollar signs filled the eyes of the chosen men who had been invited to join Alan Jellitan for this grand unveiling, to have an opportunity to get in on the ground floor of the largest money-making scheme in history.

"Vinnie Pinchey," Ronald Rat McRump whispered reverently, settling back into his seat.

"Vinnie Pinchey is the beginning of a movement," Alan explained. "Every child will want a Vinnie Pinchey doll, every woman will want to be Vinnie Pinchey, every man will want to please Vinnie Pinchey so he can own Vinnie Pinchey."

The seven men in the room with Alan Jellitan understood the concept instantly.

"Vinnie Pinchey makeup," Snarky Snellburger said, nodding his head as a creepy grin spread across his face.

"Vinnie Pinchey clothing line," John Smattering said, "and every woman and girl will have to have Vinnie Pinchey shoes and boots."

"Vinnie Pinchey home furnishings," Kenneth Shmatz said.

"Vinnie Pinchey exercise program," Ronald Rat McRump suggested.

"Vinnie Pinchey diet pills," Mark Plus said. "Women will need them in order to get that Vinnie Pinchey figure."

"Vinnie Pinchey movie, Vinnie Pinchey series, Vinnie Pinchey music."

"What about the men?" asked Jackie Patterns. "What will they be buying from us?"

"The men will be scrambling to buy the Vinnie Pinchey automobile, the Vinnie Pinchey sporting equipment, and our biggest market for men will be the Vinnie Pinchey virtual reality game," Alan said. "Men will be obsessed with it, scrambling to purchase the computer, the large screens and the giant screens, the mobile devices, the controllers, the goggles and all the accessories that will go with the game. They will travel the world to locate and take possession of the game elements."

"Vinnie Pinchey just may be our final product line," Mark Plus said, settling his plus-sized body back into his chair.

"Not maybe, Mark, but for sure," Alan Jellitan said confidently. "So, who is in?"

"I'm in," said Mark Plus instantly, clapping his hands wildly like a three-year-old.

"I am IN!" Kenneth Shmatz agreed enthusiastically.

"I am in," said the others simultaneously, all except Ronald Rat McRump, whose finances were most assuredly needed to get this project off the ground. The group looked at him expectantly.

He peaked his fingers into a power pyramid and tapped his hands together as the rest of the men held their collective breath.

"Count me in," Ronald Rat McRump said finally. "But only if I call the shots, and my participation must be kept secret, for obvious reasons. With all the right assets and aspects, I can see that Vinnie Pinchey is exactly the world needs, and what we need."

THE IMPLEMENTATION OF VINNIE PINCHEY

More than ten million Vinnie Pinchey dolls were shipped to department stores and warehouse stores several months before Christmas, coinciding with the Vinnie Pinchey series and release of the Vinnie Pinchey music video. The promised Vinnie Pinchey movie began to stir the curiosity of the public, so pre-sales of tickets were already in the billions before production even began. The online presence of Vinnie Pinchey in virtual shops and social media were the hooks and lines cast out first to the largest purchasing market in the world: pre-teen and teenage girls. Advertising for Vinnie Pinchey programming, media and merchandise flooded not only this country, but the entire world. A person could not go to a store, a city, a town, an airport, a bus station or anywhere online without having Vinnie Pinchey shoved into his face: clothing, posters, backpacks, video games, music, diet pills, even Vinnie Pinchey fast food.

Yet this flood was not only welcome, it was embraced. The consuming audience did not seem to notice nor care that the character of Vinnie Pinchey on the screen was unreal, a computer-generated image of a selfish, snooty lady with an accent that made her sound European. Vinnie Pinchey merchandise flew off the shelves immediately and the buyers demanded more and more and more. Women insisted on dressing like Vinnie Pinchey, in an attempt to look long and lean, while young girls decorated their rooms in Vinnie Pinchey fashion and hosted Vinnie Pinchey parties.

Vinnie Pinchey was subtly taking over the civilized world.

The Unraveling of the Home

Back-to-School Shopping

Sharia and Samia dashed through the mall toward their favorite department store, their pockets full of spending money. Before they arrived at that store, they were drawn off course by the clothing displays in a small specialty shop. They both stopped in their tracks, pulled by an unseen force into the store.

"Have you ever seen fashions like these?" Samia asked her older sister, as they pushed their way through the crowd that filled the store.

"Look at that sweater! I love it!" Sharia replied, grabbing a dingy green cardigan off the shelf. "And I don't even wear sweaters, well, I didn't before, not until now, as I have found the ultimate sweater for me! This is absolutely the most beautiful sweater I have ever seen in my life." She held the sweater up in front of her and examined the row of tiny dusty rose-colored buttons.

"Hey, I saw it first!" another girl shouted at her, snatching the sweater out of Sharia's hands. "This sweater is MINE!" She hugged it close to herself as she backed away with her treasure, enveloped by the crowd.

Samia saw her sister's face turn beet red, and she knew from experience, she was about to explode. She put her hand on Sharia's arm. "That one was probably not even your size."

"Are you saying I am too fat?" Sharia yelled, taking out her anger on her sister. "You think I am fat?"

"No, no, you are too tall! It would have been too short on your long torso, Shar," Samia said convincingly, well aware of her sister's obsession with her body shape and size. "Let's find one your size. That's not the only sweater in the store. I'm sure they have all sizes here. They must have a ton of different styles, too, but I'm sure they have another one like that one. Wow, every piece of clothing in this store has the same color theme." She stood on her tippy toes to get a

7

glimpse of the entire store to confirm her assumption, and she didn't see any other color on display.

"I am NOT fat!" Sharia stated.

"No, you are not at all fat, everyone can see that. You don't have to tell anyone that. Everyone can see by looking at you, you are tall, lean, and thin. All my friends want to have a body exactly like yours. I wish MY body shape could be long and lean like yours. Let's check over there. I am sure we can find a sweater like that one that is tall enough for you."

"I want THAT one," Sharia pouted, as she scanned the store for the same exact type of sweater.

"Let's go look over there," Samia suggested. "That looks like the sweater area." She picked up a blouse and skirt her size as they pressed their way through the mob of teenagers and young ladies.

Right when they arrived at the sweater section, another girl seized the final sweater of that design remaining on the table.

"Oh, I really wanted that one," Sharia complained to her sister. "I am telling you, that was the most beautiful sweater I have ever seen in my life. I have never, not ever, ever seen a more beautiful sweater, and it can't be mine. I missed it. We got here too late. I knew we should have skipped breakfast and gotten here earlier. There went my happiness, right out the window, just like that." She snapped her fingers for emphasis. "How can I ever be happy again, if I can't have that sweater?"

"Look at all the other clothes they have in here!" Samia encouraged her. She grabbed a pair of trousers, the same greeny color, that had balloon-shaped legs and bands around the ankles. "Look at these pants! They would look perfect on you! They would certainly show off your long legs."

"Yeah, if only I had that sweater to go with them," Sharia moaned. "Don't you see? That sweater would make or break my entire wardrobe! I can't believe I missed it! We were so close! I had it in my hand! I am so sure you can't even imagine how I feel right now. I mean, have you ever had such a horrible thing happen to you as this? The ultimate victory, the Holy Grail, the gold medal, was right in my hands, and just like that," she snapped her fingers again, "it was taken away from me, before I had a chance to even enjoy it for one measly little second! Can you believe it? I cannot believe it! Life is so cruel! Why does this have to happen to me? Why do I have to be the one to suffer such an awful fate? Why me? Why me?"

Samia was afraid her sister was going to break down and cry, or worse, have a temper tantrum, right there in the store, and she was way too old for that.

"Shar! Calm it down a few thousand notches! That is NOT Vinnie Pinchey," she whispered, as she massaged her sister's back, the same way their mother did those times when Sharia went off in the wrong direction mentally.

"Can I help you young ladies with something?" said a sales lady, who had materialized out of nowhere. Her voice was soothing and tranquil, exactly what Sharia needed right now.

Samia was so thankful this lady had appeared right here, right now, especially when there were at least a hundred other customers in this store she could be helping.

"My sister really likes the sweaters we saw on this table," Samia told her. "Do you by chance have another one? Someone else got the last one that was here."

"Oh, yes, this is an extremely popular style this season," she said with a smile. "This sweater has literally been flying off the shelf, if you know what I mean, especially since it was featured on Vinnie Pinchey this week."

"I knew I had seen it somewhere!" Sharia said, clapping her hands rapidly, suddenly out of her funk and giddy with excitement. "But it was not worn by Vinnie Pinchey, I know that, because I have been keeping a record on my portable device of every single thing she has been wearing, and I have lots of them already, but I know she did not wear this sweater."

"No, she did not wear this sweater," the sales lady confirmed. "When you have a chance to re-watch the program, notice the mannequin in the window of the third store she passes in the second scene is wearing the sweater."

"Oh! Oh! You are right! I remember!" Sharia exclaimed. "That is where I saw it! And even though Vinnie Pinchey was not wearing it, that sweater is so Vinnie Pinchey!"

"Indeed, it is," the sales lady agreed, nodding and smiling. "Indeed, it is."

Sharia's face fell. "I almost had it," she said. "I had it right here, in my hands, that very sweater that I love more than any sweater I have ever seen in my whole entire life, and it was taken away from me."

"Oh, don't you fret, my dear," the sales lady said, placing her hand on Sharia's forearm. "There are plenty more where that came from." As she spoke, an elderly lady with blue hair came into sight, pushing a large cart toward them overflowing with that same style of sweater. Sharia's eyes brightened as she realized her life was no longer at its lowest point.

At the Dinner Table

I was shocked to see how this Vinnie Pinchey obsession had begun to spring up around me, and I wondered why I hadn't noticed until that day in the locker room at the pool. I had seen the dolls in stores and I had noticed the ugly color themes that seemed to be taking over our town, but I had not connected the two, nor had I heard the words 'Vinnie Pinchey' before. My family had been going about our regular business, going to work and school and church, and volunteering in various capacities, as we always had done, unaware that people all over the place were becoming preoccupied with Vinnie Pinchey.

"Has anyone mentioned to you anything about Vinnie Pinchey, or have you seen anything about it on the screen?" I asked my husband, Terry, and my daughter, Zoey, as we sat at the dinner table.

"Vinnie Pinchey? What's that?" Zoey asked, shaking her soft curls. She scrunched up her nose. "It reminds me of Brussels sprouts, and they stink."

"What is that?" Terry asked, unfolding his napkin and placing it on his lap. "I've never heard of it. Or him, or her, or whatever it is." I didn't expect him to have heard of any of the latest trends, since he spent his days knee-deep in computations for a local engineering company and rarely paid attention to fads or fashions.

"Apparently, Vinnie Pinchey is some kind of a doll that has a movie and people are buying wardrobes based on this program," I said, trying to remember the facts I had read about it earlier that day. "It was the funniest thing. I was at the pool, in the locker room and getting ready to leave, and this girl, I guess she was about ten or so, started screaming her head off. I went over to see if she was all right, and she was standing there, screaming. Another girl was standing by her, watching her, and she looked like she was her sister, a couple years older, so I asked her what was wrong with her, and she said, 'She's upset because she can't have her party be Vinnie Pinchey.' So, I asked her what Vinnie Pinchey is and she looked at me like I was asking her what a car is or something. Later, when I had a few minutes, I looked up Vinnie Pinchey, and I was surprised to get more than one billion results."

"One billion results on your search?" Terry asked, pausing between bites.

"Yes, more than one billion," I said.

"That is a whole lot, isn't it, Mommy?" Zoey asked. She was only six years old, so anything over twenty was a whole lot to her.

"Yes, Zoey, it is way more than I can even imagine," I said.

"Wow," she said, clearly impressed. "I already have my doll, Monique, so I don't need another doll," she said, returning her focus to her dinner. "And Monique has her own clothes already, too."

"Well, there you have it," Terry said, adding butter to his whole wheat roll. "Our daughter has not been brainwashed by the media. We keep our eyes and our hearts on the Lord and we are not swayed by the things of the world."

"Thank God!" I said. "I'm not sure what is going on with this Vinnie Pinchey thing, but it seems to be all over the place."

"Can you do me a huge favor?" Terry asked.

"Sure, what do you need?"

"Please don't mention the words 'Vinnie Pinchey' again. Even the sound of those words is irritating, and I don't care what they mean or what it is. Whatever it is, it is not anything we need in our lives."

"I agree," I said, glad to get beyond this silly topic.

"I agree, too!" Zoey announced loudly. "I don't ever want to say it, not in my whole entire lifetime!"

"And you won't have to, Baby Girl," Terry assured her.

The Phone Call That Changed Everything

I was at work in my home office – I did accounting for several small non-profit organizations – when my phone rang. A quick glance at the caller ID told me I had to answer it, someone was calling from Zoey's school. A montage of possibilities flew through my head: Was Zoey hurt? Was she sick? Were they having a lockdown? Or – or – or? I quickly said a prayer then answered the phone.

"Yes, hello?" I said, barely taking a breath.

"Yes, are you Zoey's mother?" a nasally voice asked. I detected a hint of an accent, but couldn't tell where it might be from; anyway, that wasn't important.

"Yes, I am. Is she okay? Is she sick? Is she–"

"Please, let me finish my statement before you start blowing off in all directions," the voice said, without bothering to identify himself – or herself.

I bit my tongue in order to not reply to that rude remark about blowing off in all directions. I would definitely need to talk to this person's supervisor.

"We need you to come and pick up Zoey right now," the voice said.

"What? You need me to pick her up at school? Why?" I hoped she didn't have a fever, or was she throwing up? If she hadn't been injured, those were the two usual reasons for being called to pick up a child from school.

"Please, I must ask you to be calm and don't get yourself all in a huff, or we may need to be forced to take legal action against you," the voice said, now sounding as if she were bored with this conversation.

"Why do I need to pick up my daughter?" I demanded.

"Oh, now I see where she gets it from," the voice said, in an irritated manner.

"Gets what from?" Had I missed the point of the conversation? What was she talking about?

"The rutabaga doesn't fall far from the tree, I tell you, Miss Huffy-Puffy, so, now, before you get yourself into legal trouble, why don't I call your husband? I don't think you are the one who should be interacting with us here at the school. You need to stay away, far away from here, forever."

"Please, tell me what is going on with my daughter," I begged. I was already putting on my jacket and grabbing my car keys.

"I will not take your attitude under consideration," the voice said, and slammed the phone into the receiver, blasting out my ear.

I ran out to the car, praying all the way, to keep myself calm so as not to allow worry to enter into my thoughts. My prayers were constantly interrupted by thoughts of how rude that person on the phone had been to me. As I maneuvered through the light traffic, I kept redirecting my thoughts to prayer, because I didn't want to arrive at the school and have my anger all up in me. My poor baby, what had happened to her?

I arrived at the school and parked in a visitor parking space, about half a mile from the office, but I couldn't take a chance parking in one of the fifteen handicapped spaces, which were the only open spaces. My plan was to jog across the parking lot to the office, but my jog quickly turned into a full-speed run. I was surely breaking Olympic records, but that didn't matter. The only thing that mattered was my daughter, her health and her safety.

As I attempted to enter the door nearest the office, I tried to get control of my breathing. The door was locked. Clear on the other side of the archway, hidden from plain sight, was a call box, so I sprinted over to it and pressed the button, which made an extremely irritating beeping sound. No response. I pressed it again. Still, no response. I waited at least ten seconds before pressing it again.

I heard the weirdest sound, possibly a cross between the voice of a goose and the barking of a sea lion, and I guessed it was trying to communicate with me. "Ark-glib-eel-ee-ahb-oo?"

"I'm here to pick up my daughter," I shouted into the air, wondering if anyone could hear me.

"Goo-soo-gleep-pa-pah?" the strange sound said.

"Where is my daughter? Zoey! Where is she?" I screamed, urging my thundering heart to slow down.

"Zeep-zeep-ahb-ooo."

I didn't know what else to do, so I began pounding on the window of the door. Finally, a few minutes later, a rent-a-cop security guard who looked to be about twelve years old appeared on the other side of the door.

"I am going to call the police!" he yelled, in a voice that rivaled the reigning soprano champion, that somehow permeated through the thick glass. He stood there, safe behind the door and made a face at me, presumably an expression of anger.

"I'm here to pick up my daughter!" I shouted again, attempting a smile (which I was hoping didn't look like a scowl).

An older man – older than I was, anyway – appeared behind the security boy and it took me a few seconds to recognize him as the principal. I breathed a sigh of relief, thinking now I could find out about Zoey. He calmly pushed the door open, and I stepped forward, assuming he was opening it for me to enter, but he held it open only about an inch.

"Miss Huffy-Puffy," he said, shocking me with his use of the same phrase the person on the phone had used, "please, I must ask you to be calm and don't get yourself all in a huff, or we may need to be forced to take legal action against you."

I instantly froze. Who was writing the script for these people? I was positive that was another same phrase that person on the phone had used. In my most reserved voice, without wavering, I said, "I need to pick up my daughter."

"Oh, you are the mother of Zoey?" he asked, arching one eyebrow and giving me the once-over. "She has been expelled and we are not to allow her on school grounds ever again, not in this school, nor in any school in the district. I doubt she would ever be allowed in any school in the entire state."

"Expelled?" I shrieked, losing control of my voice. "She is six years old! What can she possibly have done to get expelled from the first grade?"

"Let us say," he said, taking the same odd tone that the person on the phone had used, "your daughter just is not Vinnie Pinchey, so she is not fit for our system of education."

"Of course, she is not Vinnie Pinchey! Her name is Zoey!"

"IF you will excuse me, I have more important matters awaiting me." He stepped back, pulling the door closed, and turned away from me. As he walked away, I noticed he actually had no hair – instead, a brown colored tattoo covered his entire head, in the fashion of a close-cut haircut.

"Where is she?" I shouted.

"Here they are!" the soprano rent-a-cop sang, pointing behind me.

I turned around and saw about fifteen police officers across the parking lot, surrounding my husband and Zoey. I leaped over to where they were in about three steps. One officer was putting handcuffs on my husband while four others held him. A female officer was holding Zoey back so she couldn't get to her daddy.

"What is going on here?" I demanded. The officers turned to me as if trying to decide if they should cuff me, too.

"That is my wife!" Terry shouted. "Zoey, go with Mommy!"

"Daddy, come with us!" Zoey cried.

"Is my husband under arrest?" I asked, stunned. Terry had never broken a single law or rule in his life. He was an engineer, after all, and he did everything by the book, exactly by the book.

"I will be home soon," he said, but his eyes betrayed him, as they swept over me as if it were the last time he would ever see me.

"Is that your mommy?" the female officer asked Zoey, narrowing her eyes at me.

"Mommy!" Zoey cried, and tears began to spill down her face.

The officer let her go, and Zoey was instantly in my arms. Terry was being forced into the back seat of the patrol car, his eyes glued to us. "I love you both so much!" he shouted, as they slammed the door, trapping him inside the car. The car zipped away, down the street and out of sight.

"Why is he being arrested?" I asked, but they acted as if they didn't even hear me. Zoey pulled me in the opposite direction.

"Don't talk to them, Mommy," she whispered.

"Why not?" I asked, watching as the patrol cars began to leave the parking lot.

Zoey shook her head, and I heard a mumbling from one of the officers.

"She is so NOT Vinnie Pinchey," he said, with a tone of disgust.

TRYING TO MAKE SENSE OUT OF NONSENSE

Zoey refused to speak during the ride home, and I was wondering how I could visit my husband, or if we needed a lawyer, and what was going on, anyway. When we arrived at home, she was not her usual bubbly self, and I still needed to find out what she had done to get expelled from school, from this district, forever. She quietly went to her room, and I followed her.

"Zoey, Sweetie, what happened at school today?" I asked.

Her eyes doubled in size and filled with tears as she looked at me.

"It's okay, Honey, I just want to know what happened."

She tucked in her lower lip and put her head down.

"What? What's the matter? I'm not going to be mad. I want to know what happened at school."

Zoey was a very bright little girl, so I knew she understood what I was saying, but was so frightened. I squatted down to be on her level, lost my balance, and tipped over. I expected her to laugh, or at least giggle, the way she always did when my clumsiness showed itself, but she still didn't look at me. I sat on the floor, watching my daughter and wondering what terrible thing had happened today that had traumatized her so.

"Come here," I said gently, reaching out my arms to her.

She took a step then fell into my lap, sobbing.

"I didn't want to say it," she spit out between sobs, then she broke down into a full four-alarm wail. I held her and rocked her, back and forth, to calm her.

I began to get angry as the possibilities flew through my brain. Had some of the kids told her to say a bad word or phrase, and she, naïve as she was, said it and then got in trouble for it? Back in my day, the teacher would have told the offender to wash his mouth out with soap, in a figurative way, but could they expel a child for such an offense? Or what else could it have been? I couldn't recall any phrases listed in the student-parent handbook that required the student to be expelled. I was certain she hadn't been dealing drugs or guns, and those were the only two violations where a student would be expelled on a first offense.

"Shhh-shhh," I said in my most soothing voice. I was holding her so close to me, hurting just about as badly as my baby was hurting, because no one should ever be able to hurt my baby like this. I needed to know what had happened, so I could go to the school or the school board and get this cleared up (and, by the way, find a lawyer and get Terry's situation cleared up as well) so Zoey could go back to school. This all had to be a big misunderstanding. First graders did not get expelled for life. Was I in the middle of one of those terrible, realistic nightmares? The circumstances said 'yes,' but the touch, the smells, the sounds said 'no.' This was actually happening to us, right now.

When she finally calmed down, I wiped her tears and kept holding her on my lap, even though I was getting sore from sitting in this position on the floor. She needed to feel safe, and this was the best way I could do that for her. She stuck her thumb into her mouth and began twirling her hair around her finger, two things she hadn't done in years. As a toddler, that had been the way she would comfort herself when she got hurt. I almost started crying then; someone had wounded my daughter. I took a deep breath and decided not to ask her any more questions until she was ready to talk about it.

My thoughts turned to my husband. Terry was the most mild-mannered, calm and reasonable person in the world. He never raised his voice, he never raised a hand to anyone. He simply listened to others and reasoned with them in a logical manner. He was always so careful to follow every rule to the letter. What possible charges could they have against him? They must have made some kind of mistake. I knew I needed to go to the police station and find out what was happening, but, on the other hand, if they gave him only one phone call, I wanted to be home to answer it. He had a cell phone, but I doubted he would be allowed to use it. Since I was at home most of the time, I didn't use one.

I glanced at our land line and could see from where we were sitting there were no messages, so that was a good thing. I had not missed his call. It had to be a mix-up. I certainly didn't understand it. What could have happened in those few minutes, between the time I had received the phone call from the rude person and the time I had arrived at the school? How did they even have time to call the police and get all of them to the school parking lot in the short time from when they called Terry after they talked to me, he drove to the school, arrived at the scene, and I arrived only a moment or two later?

My mind was looping on the insanity of the whole situation. Our daughter, the most loving, friendly, kind, obedient child in the town, had been expelled from school for an unknown reason, and my husband, the most civil and cooperative man in town had been arrested for an unknown reason, both incidents happening in a matter of minutes. Was I trapped in one of my nightmare cycles, where nothing made sense, and the sequence of events kept going forward in an illogical manner?

Zoey fell asleep in my arms, but I didn't want to set her down. I needed to feel her warmth against me in order to know that I was awake and in an actual situation. I had no idea what to do next, so I did nothing. I sat and waited, holding our daughter, smelling her hair, stroking her back gently and rocking her slowly. I was probably soothing myself as much as I was soothing her, if not more – and did I ever need some soothing at that moment.

I could have stayed in that position all day, holding my daughter, rocking her, as we comforted each other, but then the phone rang. It had to be my husband! I quickly shifted and scooted, gently setting Zoey on her bed so I could grab the phone before it went to the message machine.

"Hello! Terry?" I exhaled into the phone, eager to hear the sound of his voice, to know he was okay, this had been a mistake, I could go pick him up or he would be coming home soon.

"You are not fit to be a member of our society," a voice told me. This was definitely not my husband speaking, but, for the second time today, I was unsure if the voice on the phone was the voice of a man or a woman.

"What?" I asked, completely confused. "Who is this?"

"If I were you, I would move myself and my pitiful thing you call a family to the farthest available uninhabitable planet, so as to no longer inflict such pain on the rest of our smooth-functioning society." It sounded like the person was smacking his lips.

"I think you have the wrong number," I said, taking the phone from my ear.

"You are the one with the wrong number, Mrs. Huffy-Puffy!" the person shouted, as I placed the phone back on its charging stand.

The phone instantly rang again. I had to answer it – it might be Terry.

"Hello?" I said, using my most polite voice.

"You! Get out of here! It's people like you who are ruining everything for the rest of us!" This was not the exact same voice calling again, but it had the same intonations, the same fluctuations, the same attitude of the pervious caller.

I didn't bother to reply. I very carefully replaced the phone, in an effort to control my emotions when so many other things in my life were going out of control. Nothing was making sense today. Had I somehow stepped into Crazyland? What was going on with people today? I needed to talk to somebody about this; but I could not use the phone to call anyone and risk missing Terry's call. I really needed to talk to Terry.

I could call his cell phone! I didn't know if they had arrested him or if they had him in a holding cell, but it was worth a try. I punched in his number and waited for the line to connect. One, two, three minutes went by and his phone did not ring. I was about to end the call when I heard the ringing on the other end. One ring, then about four years before the second ring.

"Come on, come on," I whispered, tapping my foot impatiently.

"How dare you," the person who answered my husband's phone said, again, using that same type of voice that was beginning to irritate me. Was everyone trying to impersonate an extremely rude person, or what?

"I am calling to speak to my husband, Terry—"

21

"I know who you are, and I know exactly what you are trying to do, and you can be warned right now, here and now, I want this to be known and stated, right now, at this very time, and at no other, not earlier at another time, not later at another time, but right here and now while I have your undivided attention, that I know what you are trying to do, and you are not going to get away with it. It is being broadcast at this very moment, at this exact time, and everyone knows what you are trying to do, and how you are at the root of the dissatisfaction, and, frankly, we are not going to tolerate it. As a matter of fact, and you can take note of this, Miss Huffy-Puffy, if I were you, I would move myself and my pitiful thing you call a family to the farthest available uninhabitable planet, so as to no longer inflict such pain on the rest of our smooth-functioning society."

"How did you get my husband's phone?" I demanded. "Put Terry on the line!"

"Mommy?" The rising of my voice had awakened our daughter.

"How dare you," the person repeated. "I know exactly what you are trying to do, and you are not going to get away with it, I am telling you here and now. You better take this as a warning and start packing, right now."

I clicked to end the call and set the phone on the table, gently, so as not to disturb Zoey. Her big brown eyes were filled with fear as she looked at me. Tears spilled out of them as she again began to sob.

"I am so sorry, Mommy," she cried. "It's all my fault." She broke down into a sob fest, gasping for breath between sobs.

I still did not know what had happened at school, but these people who were harassing me on the phone had nothing to do with Zoey. Our home phone number must have fallen into the hands of some pranksters.

"No, Sweetie, it is NOT your fault," I said, coming over to hold her in my arms again. I wanted so badly to know what had happened at school but even more, I wanted my daughter to feel safe in my arms, in her own home.

The Neighbors Next Door

"Honey, I'm not going to the office today," Nick announced, as he waltzed into the kitchen, examining his nails.

"Are you feeling sick?" his wife, Nicole, asked. She barely looked up from her electronic tablet where she was playing the latest snack-smacking game, appropriately called 'Snack Smack.'

"No, I just don't want to go," Nick replied, leaning over to check to see if anything new was waiting for him in the refrigerator.

"Oh no!" Nicole shouted, slapping her hand down on the table. "Ow!" She didn't mean to slap it so hard.

"I want to go play golf," Nick said defensively. What he said was golf, what he meant was Vinnie Pinchey golf. Vinnie Pinchey golf was a virtual reality challenge where Nick had been spending much of his time, ever since he had purchased the interface and the module. He had not bothered to mention these expensive purchases to Nicole. With the new president in office and the new credit deregulations that he had signed into law, Nicole would not see the charges for at least ten months, since the statement now came only once a year. The ceilings on borrowing had been lifted so their credit was almost unlimited. They could take care of the frequently doubling interest rates at a much later date. They did not need to be concerned about such things as budgets and balancing at this time. Now was the time to become fully immersed in the Vinnie Pinchey life.

"Oh, it wasn't you," Nicole said. "I was almost to level 300 and I missed smacking the Ho-Ho."

"Do we have anything to eat in the house?"

"I don't know, I don't feel like eating, so I don't feel like cooking so I don't feel like shopping," Nicole said, starting another game. She would have to completely concentrate for the next hour or so if she wanted to get beyond level three hundred.

"Well, it's good for you to skip a few meals," Nick stated.

Nicole nodded. In the past, she would have taken his remark as an insult, but now she realized what he was saying was true. She would have to skip quite a few meals since her main goal in life now was Vinnie Pinchey, and to be all Vinnie Pinchey, she would have to lose a lot of weight. "Did you take your Vinnie Pinchey diet pills?"

Nicole was taken aback. "Vinnie Pinchey would never need to be on a diet! They are not diet pills!"

"Oh, oops, if I may beg your pardon," Nick said, giving a little bow.

"You may beg."

"What I meant to ask you, did you take your Vinnie Pinchey supplements?"

"Yes, thank you for checking. I did take them already, earlier this morning."

"And the kids, did they have anything?" Nick wanted a little something else to eat, anything left over, but he knew he could not afford to gain any weight.

"Of course! They had their Vinnie Pinchey shakes. They won't be getting hungry for quite some time. By the way, if I may ask of you a favor."

"You may ask," Nick said, adding, "but I cannot guarantee I will be able to do anything for you. My day is booked pretty solid."

"My Vinnie Pinchey supplements are getting low. Can you pick up another batch from the store while you are out?"

"No, I don't feel like doing that today. Can't you go and get them?"

"No, I don't feel like going anywhere today," Nicole answered. "Don't worry about it. It's okay, I can have them delivered." She didn't mind paying the enormous delivery fee.

"Do I hear the kids upstairs?" Nick asked, settling for a whole wheat muffin with a thin spread of peanut butter. In order to be the type of man for Vinnie Pinchey, he himself could not afford to gain any weight.

"Yeah, they didn't feel like going to school," Nicole answered, unconcerned.

"Why should they?" Nick asked, following his muffin with two large glasses of water. "The teachers are so behind the times. What can they teach our kids that can't be learned from Vinnie Pinchey?"

"My thoughts exactly," Nicole said, successfully smacking two snacks at once.

"Mom!" Samia called from upstairs. "I can't find my Vinnie Pinchey doll!"

"It is in the place where you last left it," Nicole said, immediately realizing her mistake. "She! She! She is in the place where you left *her*!" she called, hoping in her error she had not been irreverent to Vinnie Pinchey.

The house felt like it was being rumbled by a stampede as Nick Jr., Sharia and Samia thundered down the steps.

"Rats!" Nicole said, taking note of the time. She would not have a chance to get to the next level of Snack Smack this morning, because Vinnie Pinchey was coming on the giant screen in a couple of minutes. She threw her tablet on the table and dashed into the other room, settling on the couch next to the girls.

"My golf game can wait," Nick said, adding his dirty dishes to the pile in the sink. He did not want to miss this episode of Vinnie Pinchey. This program was top priority in his family, and in a large majority of families across the nation. How had anyone been able to function before the introduction of Vinnie Pinchey?

The family snuggled in the viewing room, ready to learn their next directions from Vinnie Pinchey.

"Oh, good you found her," Nicole said to Samia, who was cradling her Vinnie Pinchey like a baby.

"She is not a baby!" Nick Jr. shouted at his sister, suddenly aware of how Vinnie Pinchey was being held.

"I want to cuddle her," Samia said, defiantly hugging her Vinnie Pinchey and moving back and forth with her doll in her arms.

"Vinnie Pinchey definitely does NOT need any cuddling," Nick Jr. said.

"But she said I can do whatever I want," Samia said, sticking out her lower lip.

"Well, it is true that Vinnie Pinchey said that, but she didn't mean to HER," Sharia said. "And Vinnie Pinchey would never pout."

Samia instantly pulled in her lower lip and put her Vinnie Pinchey into a sitting position on her lap. She could cuddle her Vinnie Pinchey later, when no one was watching, but her brother and sister were probably right, Vinnie Pinchey could not be cuddled in front of other people. Besides, right now Vinnie Pinchey would want to watch her own program, wouldn't she?

The opening scene of Vinnie Pinchey showed her walking on a sidewalk in a big city, her pointy nose in the air, oblivious to the crowds who were surrounding her, staring up at her, imitating her, as she towered head and shoulders above the rest of the people. She carried a dusty rose-colored bag and wore shoes to match. Her plain dress was the ugliest color of green imaginable, hanging loosely around her pencil-thin body. Nicole and Sharia took mental notes on the fashions of Vinnie Pinchey – they were straightway THE clothes to wear, the shoes to wear, the bags to carry, the only kind of things to be seen wearing and carrying outside of the house. Sharia had already tossed out all of her clothes that didn't fit into the Vinnie Pinchey color scheme, leaving her closet nearly empty. Nicole had not yet been so ambitious as to throw away her clothes that were out of compliance with Vinnie Pinchey, but she had piled them up on the floor of her closet so she wouldn't accidentally wear them. She would need to get into Samia's closet and do the same, to make sure Samia would not embarrass the family when they left the house together. Poor little girl, she still thought it was acceptable to wear yellow and blue.

Nick glanced at his family, all glued to the screen, hanging on every word, every phrase, every mannerism, every behavior and every action of Vinnie Pinchey. He was so proud of his family and the way they were all growing together, with the same Vinnie Pinchey values, the same Vinnie Pinchey ideas, the same Vinnie Pinchey ambitions. As far as he was concerned, they were learning everything they needed, right here and now. What more important things could his children possibly learn at school?

Unthinkable Answers

Two days had passed since my husband had been arrested and our daughter had been expelled from school, and I still didn't have any answers to either situation. Zoey was following me around the house like a puppy, afraid to let me out of her sight, and she, my normally talkative little girl, acted as if she were afraid to speak, keeping her mouth plugged with her thumb. I was getting accustomed to the bizarre phone calls, since they were coming every few minutes. I had to answer the phone; I needed to hear from Terry. I had called the police station three times, only to get more of the same rhetoric that was coming to me through the phone calls, along with threats that if I continued to call the station, I would be arrested for harassing the police!

I needed to get to work at my computer, for my clients, since I had no idea whether my husband still had a job. We still had bills to pay, we still had a mortgage to keep current, and we still needed to buy food. I had received a notice in the mail that Terry's car had been towed from the school parking lot and was being held in the city impound lot. The fine was already well over seven thousand dollars, with another thousand being added daily, and the ten-year-old car was only worth about three thousand dollars. I was unable to do anything about that car at this point, so I had to let it go. We still had our economy car, the one I usually drove, safe inside our garage.

I reluctantly went into my office with Zoey right behind me, sucking her thumb and dragging her favorite blanket. As I flopped down in my chair at the desk, she plopped down on her blanket on the floor, her dark round eyes glued to me. I could see she was afraid she might lose me, the same irrational way she had lost her daddy and her life at school.

A wave of guilt crashed over me as I realized I needed to be her school teacher, starting immediately. Zoey was a smart little girl, already able to read before she started first grade, and I needed to feed that growing brain with information.

"Sweetie, here is a book you can read," I said, handing her a book. She stared at me without responding.

"Zoey, did you hear what I said? You love this book." I held out the colorful book with the orange cat on the front, one of her favorites, the book that had inspired her to want to learn to read when she was only two, but she didn't even look at it. She reminded me so much of herself as a baby that I had to look away from her so I wouldn't start crying. Where was my big girl, my growing girl, my daughter who was always so eager to learn and advance?

I sat on the floor beside her with the book in my hand. "Do you want me to read it to you? You love Punkin the Kitty."

She rolled over on the floor so her head was on my lap, but she was not looking in the direction of the book.

"Come on, Sweetie, you are a big girl," I said soothingly. "I am going to be your teacher now, and this is your school."

She started to cry.

I stroked her hair. "It's okay, Zoey. We are here together."

"I don't have any friends," she mumbled around her thumb, which was still in her mouth.

"Sure, you do," I said, trying to convince her and myself, too. I didn't know any of the little girls at school – Zoey had only been going there for ten days – and I wondered about my own friends as well. I had left messages for JoAnn and Lori and Kim the day Terry had been arrested, but they hadn't returned my calls. I was trying to recall the name of any of her classmates Zoey had mentioned, but could not think of even one.

"Who is that girl you played with on the first day of school?" I asked, reaching for her to give me a name.

"They all hate me," Zoey said, in the most downtrodden voice I had ever heard her use.

"Zoey, we don't use the word 'hate,' you know that, and I am positive the girls in your class do not feel that way about you. They like you."

28

"No, they don't," she said, starting to cry again. I recalled my own childhood as a very shy little girl, and the times I had thought girls hated me because they didn't reach out to me, but Zoey was not shy. She easily made friends with everyone, due to her bright smile and sunshiny personality. "You told me the other day you were making lots of new friends."

"That was before they all told me they hate me!" She buried her face in her hands.

"They said that to you? Why would anybody talk to you like that? You are so friendly to everyone."

"They said that to me because I told them the truth," she said, crying even harder now.

"What do you mean? What did you tell them?" I silently prayed she hadn't told a little girl she was fat or had a big nose or anything like that.

"I'm sorry, Mommy, I didn't want to say it, but I couldn't help it," she confessed.

"What did you say?" I was holding my breath, almost afraid to hear the word she thought was causing her little friends to turn against her.

"THAT word," Zoey said, as if I knew what word she was thinking of.

"Which word?"

"I am not supposed to say it," she said, "ever."

She was so young, she only knew a few words we had told her never to use.

"What did you say? It's okay, you can say it to me now and you won't be in trouble. I promise."

She looked at me as if she might not trust my promise. She shook her head. "I can't say it again. Ever."

"What is it, Sweetie? What letter does it start with?"

"It starts with the letter..." she paused, and I could see the alphabet running through her mind. "I don't know."

"What does this letter sound like?"

"It's two words. Like 'vip.' It sounds like 'vip,' but I know there is not a letter named vip."

"Does it start with 'v,' could that be it?"

"Yes, only not vee, but vip, and also hay."

"Hay? The letter 'h,' like ha?"

"But not ha, it's like hay."

I scanned my memory for words that started with the letter 'v' or 'h' that Zoey was not to use.

"Did you tell any of the kids they are going to go to hell?" I asked, knowing that religion was a very touchy subject in the schools, and it possibly could get her suspended if she said the wrong thing.

"NO!" she yelled, visibly shocked I would even use that 'h' word at all, much less in that context.

"Zoey, I need to know what you said," I said, trying to be firm and loving at the same time.

"Promise you won't get mad at me?" she asked, looking up at me, searching my eyes for the truth.

"I promise I won't get mad at you," I said, nodding once.

"Okay, if you promise."

"Yes, I promise."

"I said the word..." she was so quiet, I could barely hear her little voice. "I said, I haaay..."

"What? What are you saying? I couldn't hear you."

"I haaaay..." she said again, cautiously, quietly.

"You haaaay..." I asked. "What does that mean?"

"I said 'I hate'!" she shouted.

"Honey, why did you say that at school?" I was truly confused at this point. Did some little girl say she hated Zoey because Zoey had said it first to her, or to one of Zoey's friends? "We never tell anyone we hate someone."

"I didn't!" she protested.

"Then what did you say to make all this trouble?"

She began crying again. "I am not supposed to say it! Ever!"

"I'm sorry, Sweetie, but I need to know. You can tell me. Tell me the whole thing." I hugged her close to me as I tried to figure out what was going on in her mind, and how that had triggered her being expelled from school.

"I told them…" she said between sniffles, "I hate Vinnie Pinchey. There. I said it." She looked up at me and pressed her lips tightly together.

"And then what happened?" I asked, wondering how this statement could have escalated into Zoey being permanently expelled from the entire school district.

"Everyone in my class said they hate me and my teacher got really mad at me and told me to go to the office and the office lady told me you were coming to pick me up and then Daddy came to the office and the principal talked to him and Daddy yelled that the school was breaking the law and the principal laughed at him and then the police came and took Daddy outside and I followed them and then you came and the police took Daddy in the police car."

"What else did your teacher say? Before she told you to go to the office, before you said what you said?"

"All the kids in my class were talking about how much they love that thing I –" she stopped herself before she said the forbidden word again, "the thing I do not like even one little bit. All the kids in my class only want to wear ugly green clothes and dirty red shoes, and I don't want to wear those ugly colors because my favorite colors are bright pink and purple and I don't want to change my favorite colors when everybody says I have to like their ugly green and dirty red. I love purple, Mommy!" She threw her hands around my neck and buried her face in my chest.

"I know you do, Sweetie, and so do I. You can like whatever color you want, and you don't have to like any color you think is ugly. You have a free choice to like your own favorite colors. Nobody can tell you what color to like."

31

This Vinnie Pinchey thing was becoming much more complicated than I had dreamed it could possibly be. I wanted to call the school again, or call the police station again, but perhaps I needed to do a little research first. The entire community could not have gone senseless over a Vinnie Pinchey craze, could they have??? Because of Vinnie Pinchey, my whole family was in trouble.

On the Other Side of the State

Julia was carefully choosing her food from the long line of potluck dishes at the company picnic. Everything looked good, but she had to be careful about what she ate.

With only a hamburger and a few vegetables on her plate, she went to stand under one of the shelters at the park. She set her plate on the table and was about to pick up her hamburger when she was surprised to see the new president of the nation walking towards her. His wispy hair was flapping in the wind, and she wondered again what color it actually was. Today, in the daylight, it looked strangely greenish. Usually on the screen, it looked either yellow or orange. In any case, this could not be a natural color. She decided he must be involved with the new movement across the country, where everybody was loving the ugliest green color.

"I see you got some food," he said, looking at her plate and stating the obvious.

"Yes, did you get some?" She was very nervous and she didn't know what to say. She wondered where the Secret Service people were. She knew they must be hiding among the crowd watching the president and his interactions.

"Oh, no, I never eat this kind of common food," he said snobbishly. "It certainly is a beautiful day, and you are a very beautiful woman." He looked her up and down, glaring at her body.

She was upset that the country had selected a womanizer as the new president, and she did not feel at all flattered. With every word he spoke, she felt as if he were trying to manipulate her. He did not bother to ask her name.

"Yes, it is a beautiful day," she agreed, ignoring the remark about herself.

He moved his hand over onto hers, as she had it sitting on the table beside her plate, and he grabbed her fingers, gently. She looked down and noticed his fingers were very stubby and rougher than she would imagine for a man who never did any kind of work. His fingers were not any longer than a child's fingers, but he was at least a foot taller than she was.

She realized this was probably the only opportunity she would ever have to speak to this man, and she didn't know if she could make a difference, but she decided to try. Before she could open her mouth to speak, he began a speech.

"I completely like the direction the country is going since I have taken over, and this country is going to be very great again, before you even know it. We can already see the signs of it happening now."

She was not impressed by his bragging, and she built up her courage to speak to him frankly. Her heart was pounding tremendously, beating savagely in her chest, and she knew her face must be turning all shades of red.

"You have to love the way people are taking care of their own business now, not bothering other people, and making themselves better people in our country," he said, using a tone that was inappropriately sexy.

She again glanced around, searching to be rescued by the invisible Secret Service men who were constantly guarding the President.

"Mr. President, I hope you don't mind if I speak frankly to you."

"Oh, no, please, go ahead. A beautiful woman like you can say anything to me." He wiggled his eyebrows up-and-down and gave her the creepiest smile she had ever seen. He squeezed her fingers slightly.

Julia became aware of other people from her job looking at them from a distance, and she wanted to pull her hand away from his clammy fingers; but she could not. She also knew she had to speak to him right now. She had only one chance.

"So, what I was going to ask you, what I've been wondering," she began nervously.

He interrupted her before she could say what she meant to say. "Are you going to ask me, 'what is a nice guy like me is doing in a place like this?' Well, I am telling you right now, you and I could get out of here, together, and we wouldn't be here."

"Actually, I was going to ask you question of a completely different sort, a completely different topic," she said, attempting to take a deep breath. She tried to pull her hand away, but his grip was too tight.

"Well, fire away, my little beauty," he said, leering at her. "I have nothing but answers for you, you can ask me anything you like, and with your beautiful features and your beautiful eyes looking at me, how could I say anything but yes?"

She was disgusted by his remarks, but she did not tell him so. Instead, she asked her question.

"Mr. President, I would like to ask, in your plan for our country, you would consider the poorest people of our nation. I have read your economic plan completely, and I see you have no plans to help them. As a matter of fact, you want to take away the benefits they are getting. Do you have any plans to help anybody except the very rich in this country?"

"Well, my first answer would be that you should speak to my economic adviser, because I am not qualified to speak on those terms. But I can tell you this one thing for sure. Poor people are poor because they made themselves poor. It is their own fault they are poor, and all they have to do is make more money and they can be rich. Why in the world would I want to help a poor person continue to be poor? I cannot support that type of behavior, and our country simply has no place for poor people. This is a country for the rich, and the very rich, and the extremely rich. Those are the only three classes of people our government needs to support. So, my answer to you is, yes, I am helping somebody besides the very rich in our country. The plans include assistance for the rich, for the very rich, and for the extremely rich. Those three categories will each get great a financial boost so the rich can become very rich, and the very rich can become extremely rich, and extremely rich can become insanely rich."

"How can you say being poor is a person's own fault? If a person is born a poor, he has no advantage, and for the most part, people who are poor when they are born are poor all of their lives. You have taken away the opportunities for poor people to get financial aid and other assistance to go to college, so how can a person who is poor ever get out of that category?"

"My dear, I don't know why you are worrying your beautiful little self about this matter. Were you not listening to me? A person does not have to stay poor. All he has to do is get money, lots of money, and he will become rich.

"Take this example. A person wants to be a millionaire, so he gets a million dollars. He wants to be a billionaire, so he gets a billion dollars. It's that simple. The money multiplies up from there. But I know pretty girls like you are not very good at math, so you can't understand the multiplication factor in business."

She was fuming under the collar, but she had to continue the conversation.

"Mr. President, with all due respect, you can't blame a person who is poor who had to spend all his money on medical bills, because he has a medical condition. Maybe he has huge hospital bills, and now he has lost everything, his house, his car, his job, because of the condition. You can't blame a person for being poor, so how would you help that person, since you have taken away his medical insurance?"

"Oh, my pretty little thing, you really are worrying way too much. I don't like to see those worry lines on your face. If you keep worrying like this, you won't stay pretty like you are now.

"Obviously, you did not read the plan well enough to know that if this guy had the best medical insurance in the first place, he would not lose everything. As a matter of fact, with the best medical insurance plans, a person who is sick can come out financially better than when he was well. That's the kind of plan I have, and I pay for it, to keep it that way. On the other hand, if a person is very sick, he should go ahead and die. We don't need sicklings in our great country. They just make trouble and problems for all of us."

"Except for the doctors and hospitals and insurance companies who are getting rich from his treatment," she mumbled.

"Well, you see? That is exactly what I am talking about here. The rich are becoming more rich, so the rich will become very rich, and the very rich will become extremely rich, and the extremely rich will become insanely rich. Isn't ours a beautiful system?"

"What about somebody who is poor because he lost everything in a house fire? You can't blame everybody who is poor for being poor.

I will admit, some have made bad choices, but not everybody who is poor made bad choices."

"Why do bad things happen to good people? The answer is, if a person is truly good, bad things will not happen to that person. Only good things happen to truly good people. If a person had a house fire, the house burned down and he lost all those possessions, then he can collect the insurance money, and hopefully, he bought more insurance money than he needed to cover his house full of possessions, and now he's better off than he was before, because he has a brand-new house, and all brand-new possessions to fill it.

"So, my little pretty one, let's get out of here and go to a place where we can be alone and have a much friendlier conversation." He pulled her hand over to his chest. She tried to get it back, but he was holding onto it tightly. She glanced around, but, unfortunately, nobody was watching them at this time. She was so frustrated, because this park was filled with people; so, how could nobody be looking at the president of the country? What if she were going to do him harm? Would there not be any witnesses? The bigger question was, what if he were going to do her harm? Then there would not be any witnesses.

"Well, Mr. President, what about this scenario; and this happened to my mother. She had insurance on her house, plenty of insurance, but she lives in the desert. So, when her house flooded, and she needed to replace furniture and other items, and she needed to have portions of the house rebuilt, and cleaned up, the insurance didn't cover it because they don't provide flood insurance if you live in the desert."

"How could a house be flooded in the desert? You are being ridiculous, and making up impossible scenarios. I genuinely don't know why a pretty young woman like you is worrying about all of these kinds of things. I'm sure you have much more important things to think about, like keeping your figure, and where to buy beautiful clothes like those you are wearing now."

"Her house flooded because her neighbor's sprinkler system broke, and water flooded her basement. So, she had to pay nearly $40,000 to get the house cleaned up and restored to its original condition, and all the items inside were lost, because the insurance wouldn't cover a flood."

"Well, it sounds like a lawsuit to me. She should end up better than she was at the beginning, like in the other cases I stated. Young lady, you are making me think so hard. I have not done this much thinking since I spent those three months in community college way back: how long ago was it? Forty years? Fifty years? Ha-ha, that was the hardest I ever had to work in my life. I'm telling you, I am so smart! Look at me! I am the smartest man you have ever met! I have never had to work a day in my life, except for that one experimental time when I did go to community college. And the only thing I learned from my experimental experience was that it was a big mistake, so I really can't recommend college for anyone.

"I am putting in a proposal for all the colleges to close down, so we can build brand new business schools and training centers in their place, where students, young people and old people, can learn to be good businessmen like I am. Those are the type of people we need in this country, so the rich can become very rich and the very rich can become extremely rich and the extremely rich can become insanely rich.

"How old do you think I am anyway? Look at me. Look at this face. Look at my eyes. How old do you think I am?

"Mr. President, with all due respect, I know how old you are because it was in the media. You are the oldest president we have ever elected." She did not want to look at his face, and especially into those beady little eyes. He reminded her of some kind of a rodent, and she was beginning to feel ill.

"But I look a lot younger than I actually am, don't you think? Come on, pretty baby, look at me. Darling, I can tell you want me. Don't you think I'm the best looking man around? And how much surgery do you think I have had on my face? Can you see any little lines? Can you see any scars? Look at me, look at this body. This is the body of a young, healthy man, and it can be all yours, today."

Julia really wanted to throw up, and to pull her hand away from him and run away from him as fast as she could, but he had a tight grip on her.

"Mr. President, with all due respect, this has been an interesting conversation, but I need to go now."

She tried without success to step away from him. He pulled her even closer to himself, nauseating her even more.

"But my darling, where could you possibly go that would be more interesting, more exciting, more wonderful than being with me? Don't you know, I can give you everything you want? I can give you everything, all of me today, and I can give you everything you want for the rest of your life. Are you in the category of rich? I can move you up to the category of the very rich with the snap of my fingers, one word from my lips.

"Speaking of my lips, they would truly love to taste your lips right now."

He tried to pull her closer to him, but she resisted. She knew he had had other women put in jail for resisting him, but she couldn't stand him. He was the essence of sleaze. She definitely did not want to get close enough to breathe his body odor. The cologne he was wearing smelled like insect repellent, and she did not want to get any closer to him.

"No, thank you, Mr. President, but I really do need to leave right now."

"I know when you say, 'no,' you mean, 'yes,' my little pretty one. The more you try to pull away from me, the more I want you. You know you're doing that to me. That's what you women do, pretend you don't want us men, and then you make us want you more and more. I know what you are doing. I have seen these tactics before. I know you want me. Look at me."

She did not want to look at him. She wanted to get far away from him.

"Mr. President, when I say 'no,' I mean 'no.' Now, would you kindly release my hand, so I can leave?"

He had a twinkle in his eye. "I know what you mean. I know, I know. You say 'no,' but I do know."

"I don't think you do know, but when I say, 'no,' that is what I mean. No."

"But you have not eaten your food?"

"I don't have an appetite anymore. I need to get going now."

"Well it's no problem, I can take you to get the best food in town, or we can get on my private plane and I can take you to get the best food in this country, or in any country. It's okay, you don't need a passport. You say the word, and we will be on our way, together."

"Mr. President, where is your wife?"

"My wife doesn't have anything to do with us. This is just between you and me. And I am so glad to be here with you today, right here, right now. You have made my whole day. You don't know how long I have been searching for somebody exactly like you. Come on. Let's get out of here. Together." He put his free hand between her legs, making her jump away from him.

"No, thank you, and I don't appreciate you making decisions for me."

She tugged on her hand to pull away from him, but he gripped it even tighter.

"Hey! I am the president! I am in charge of everyone and everything! I can tell anybody and everybody what to do! And you have to do what I say, everything I say, because I am the president. You can't say 'no' to me. Do you know what happens to people who say 'no' to me?"

"Yes, you are the president, but you are not a dictator. The last I checked this is still a free country."

The president burst out in laughter. "Nothing is free, especially not this country! Everything has a price! Everything has a cost! You know, the rich will become very rich and the very rich will become extremely rich and the extremely rich will become insanely rich. And if you don't go with me now, you are going to get a taste of that price, and you will not fall in any of these categories. You will be in the category of the imprisoned, the poor, the dead."

"Is that a threat, Mr. President? Are you threatening me? Are you saying we cannot agree to disagree on this?" she asked, trying hard to pull away from this disgusting man. She was beginning to be very afraid, afraid she would have to do whatever he said because he was the president.

"My little beauty, I think we are going to get along just fine. I like

40

feisty women, especially when they are as beautiful as you are." He began to kiss the top of her head while she tried, unsuccessfully, to get away from him.

Suddenly, she and the president were surrounded by men dressed in black, and they were ushered to a bank of limousines idling at the edge of the park. She tried to pull away, but one of the men put his arms around her and his hand over her mouth so she couldn't make a sound. She could not believe it! She was being kidnapped by the president of the country!

THE FAMILY ACROSS THE STREET

Karen didn't feel like fixing dinner for her husband, Darrell, and their daughter, Darlene, but she knew if she didn't prepare something for them, they would not eat. They were both so involved with their Vinnie Pinchey lives, neither of them had any kind of appetite anymore. The only thing financially keeping them in this house was that Darrell loved his job as a firefighter, so he kept going to work every week. He was at home today, he didn't have another shift for a couple of days, and he was deeply involved with his Vinnie Pinchey virtual reality game. She could see him through the back window, out in the yard with his Vinnie Pinchey headset on, swinging his Vinnie Pinchey sword at enemies only visible to him. The headset fit him so much better since he had shaved his head and had the Vinnie Pinchey hair tattooed onto his scalp.

Karen was struggling with resisting Vinnie Pinchey. Her friends and family were already so enraptured by the movement, Karen could only hope it was merely a passing phase, they would grow out of it, get beyond it and move on to something else that was not all-consuming. The family watched Vinnie Pinchey together, a bonding activity, and Karen admired Vinnie Pinchey and how she had everything in her life together and under her control. Vinnie Pinchey never did anything she didn't want to do. People respected and appreciated Vinnie Pinchey, and with good reason. Vinnie Pinchey was the absolute ideal woman in her looks, her fashion sense, her mannerisms, her attitude. Karen did want to be more Vinnie Pinchey, but she also wanted to retain her own physical characteristics and her own way of talking. This had already cost her some of her friendships, but then, had they actually been her friends? They had certainly jumped ship when something better was on the horizon, or, rather, something more Vinnie Pinchey.

"Mom!" Darlene shouted, stomping into the room. "Mom! Why did you not answer me? I called you!"

"Now, Dear, you are not sounding Vinnie Pinchey right now,"

Karen said, using the only strategy that worked with her teenager these days.

Darlene calmed herself and lowered her voice, holding her head high, nose in the air, just like Vinnie Pinchey. "Look at this," she said, thrusting her mobile device into Karen's face.

Karen looked, unsure of what she was expected to see. She nodded noncommittally.

"This is the OLD version of Vinnie Pinchey!" Darlene cried.

"The old version?"

"Yes, and you have to unlock my credits so I can get the new version! How can I follow along and keep up if I don't have the new version? I am going to be kicked out of school like the girl across the street!" She stood firm and set her jaw against her mother.

"The little girl across the street got kicked out of school?" Karen asked. This was news to her. She had never even made an effort to meet the neighbors – who did, in times such as these? Every family needed to take care of its own and not get into the business that was going on with anyone else. People today did not have the time or resources to be distracted by others who were outside of the circle of importance.

"Yes, and I probably will, too!" Darlene pouted; then her face brightened. "But actually, I don't need to go to school, do I? Lots of kids don't go anymore, since we can learn everything we need to know from Vinnie Pinchey."

"Oh, no, you are not getting out of school to do your Vinnie Pinchey thing all day. Besides, they do teach Vinnie Pinchey at school, don't they? It is the core subject, isn't it?"

"It's not a Vinnie Pinchey *thing*!" Darlene protested. "It is Vinnie Pinchey. I want to be all Vinnie Pinchey." Her demeanor relaxed and she instantly took on the poise and position of Vinnie Pinchey.

"So... the little girl across the street got kicked out of school because her mobile device was not up to date with Vinnie Pinchey?" Karen asked.

"I don't know about that part, but I heard she did get kicked out –

permanently, and so, she can never, ever come back to our school district, thank Vinnie Pinchey, because she..." Darlene lowered her voice reverently, "... I heard she said she hates..."

"She got expelled from school because she hates?" Karen asked. "I don't get it. I mean, I know Vinnie Pinchey does not hate anything or anyone, but I don't understand."

"Mom!" Darlene said, again raising her voice. "You don't get it!"

"No, I don't. Why don't you explain it to me?" Now Karen was beginning to get irritated, and she doubted she would be able to maintain a Vinnie Pinchey tone of voice for much longer. She again used that tactic in an attempt to keep her daughter in control. "What would Vinnie Pinchey say? Or, I should ask, how would Vinnie Pinchey say it?"

Darlene took a deep breath, again pointing her nose in the air. When she began to speak, her voice was measured and precise. "The little girl across the street was permanently removed from our school system because she has no respect for Vinnie Pinchey." She lowered her voice and looked to the left and right, to be sure someone had not sneaked into the house to overhear the conversation. "I heard she actually said she hates Vinnie Pinchey."

Karen gasped, shocked that a young child would so boldly defy everything that was being put into place. She herself was not completely on board with every aspect of Vinnie Pinchey, but she certainly could not condone such blatant rebellion. Darlene was pinching her face together, the stress showing as bright as the sun.

"Well, I should say, I must ask you to be calm and don't get yourself all in a huff," Karen said in her best Vinnie Pinchey voice. She attempted to imitate a Vinnie Pinchey expression.

Darlene's face immediately relaxed at the tone of her beloved Vinnie Pinchey words of reassurance.

"Yes, my dear mother, you are absolutely correct," Darlene replied, sounding like a completely different person. "The actions of others, although they be atrocious, need not affect us directly when they are not directed toward us directly."

Karen recognized the Vinnie Pinchey phrase, and she was proud of how her daughter had been able to channel the emotions and take control of her own reactions. This was another benefit they could attribute to Vinnie Pinchey, another value added to the family and to the society in which they resided.

A large crash in the back yard got their attention. Darrell apparently had gotten too close to one of the trees. He was lying on the ground, his Vinnie Pinchey sword beside him, and a large tree branch on top of him.

Karen and Darlene began to laugh loudly at the humorous sight.

"Look at Dad!" Darlene said, doubling over in laughter. "I know he really tries so hard, but that is so NOT Vinnie Pinchey!"

Karen was caught up in amusement for a couple of minutes, but when she realized Darrell was not moving, a sense of panic came over her. That branch on top of him was quite large. He might need help. She tried to think of whom she could call to come over to the house and provide some assistance, but no names or faces came to her mind. She and Darlene were the only ones available. They probably should move quickly.

"Darlene, we need to go out and see if Dad needs some help," Karen said, still trying to imitate Vinnie Pinchey fluctuations in her voice.

"I don't want to go outside," Darlene complained. "It looks like it is super cold out there, and I don't have on the right kind of clothes. Hey, that reminds me, did you buy my Vinnie Pinchey coat? You promised you would buy me a Vinnie Pinchey coat! I can't go outside wearing colors like this! Hardly any items in my wardrobe are Vinnie Pinchey! I need a whole new wardrobe! You have to go and get it for me today! I can't go back to school wearing the same old Vinnie Pinchey clothes I have already been wearing!"

Karen ignored Darlene's whining and rushed through the mud room and out the back door, keeping her eyes on Darrell. He hadn't moved one bit since they had heard the loud crash.

"Mom! Do you hear me? Are you listening to me?" Darlene yelled from the kitchen, as the door slammed behind Karen. "Nobody ever ignores Vinnie Pinchey!"

"Darrell! Are you okay?" Karen called, as she ran to her husband. The tree branch was a lot bigger than it looked from the kitchen, and it looked like it was crushing her husband. "Can you hear me? Are you hurt?"

"Kleee a boydo," Darrell mumbled.

Karen tried to lift the branch, but it was too heavy. She heaved and pulled, and was not able to move it. From here, she could see Darrell still had on his virtual reality headset, so she didn't know if he could see her or the tree, or not. He could be looking at a completely different landscape and have no idea that a huge tree branch had landed on top of him.

"Can you breathe?" Karen asked, worried sick about him. If she could not move the branch, she would need to call emergency services. Although it may be necessary to call them and have them come to help, that would be completely contrary to anything Vinnie Pinchey, which could mean trouble for her family.

"Kleee a boydo," Darrell repeated.

"What are you saying?" Karen asked more loudly. "I can't understand you! Darrell! I cannot understand a word you are saying!"

"Kleee a boydo," Darrell said, his voice even lower than it had been.

Karen was beginning to panic. Her husband was lying there, crushed, on the ground, and now he was talking nonsense. She could only hope he was responding to something in his Vinnie Pinchey virtual reality. She kept trying to move the branch off of him, but she did not have enough strength.

She didn't dare ask any of the neighbors for help; that would put her family at the lowest rung on the Vinnie Pinchey ladder. Since the new administration had taken over and Vinnie Pinchey was becoming the norm in this country, people did not think about others. The whole attitude of Vinnie Pinchey was to do whatever you wanted all the time and forget about the needs and desires of others. Of course, some people still WANTED to help others, like her husband, a firefighter, and some doctors who were still practicing; and there were still a few Vinnie Pinchey resistors, those who, for some unexplainable reason, did not want to partake in Vinnie Pinchey, who still held onto those ancient values, like helping people and being generous, but Karen didn't know any of them personally.

"Darrell, stay there, and I am going to call one of your buddies at the fire department. Who should I ask for? We just need one very strong person to help me lift this branch off of you."

"NOOOO!" he shouted. "Kleee a boydo, pleee."

Karen tried to move closer to him, pushing smaller branches away from her so she could get near him.

"It's going to be okay," she said, reaching for him, to comfort him.

"Keep... your... voice... down," he whispered loudly. "You... shout... is... so... not... Vinnie Pinchey."

"Oh, that's what you were saying," Karen said, suddenly comprehending. He did not want her to embarrass him by letting anyone know he was currently not in complete control. "Well, are you aware that you are in our back yard and a huge branch fell on you, and you are currently being crushed by it? And it is so heavy, still attached to the tree, that I am unable to move it off of you by myself? I need to get some help."

"Dar...lene," he said, struggling to speak. "Help... you."

"Darlene does not want to come outside right now," Karen said. "She doesn't have the right Vinnie Pinchey jacket, and she doesn't feel like coming out of the house. She is working on getting her Vinnie Pinchey attitude just right."

"Oh, yes... give... her... that," Darrell said. "Do... not... bother... her."

"Do you want me to remove the headset?" Karen offered.

"I... need... it," he said. "I... am... so... far... be... hind."

"What should I do? How can I get you out of this mess?"

"Please... do... not... tell..." he begged.

"You don't want me to tell anyone what happened to you? Okay, I won't, but we need to get you out of here. I can't do it by myself."

"Chain... saw," he suggested, his voice barely a whisper now.

47

"What? No! I am not going to try to cut this branch with a chain saw! You know I can't even lift the enormous chain saw you have in the garage. And even if I could lift it, do you think I would risk using it right here, with you lying on the ground, there? Oh, no, I'm not even going to try it."

Darrell did not reply. Karen looked around and noticed it would be getting dark soon. She had to do something, Vinnie Pinchey or not. She had to get some help. She had to call someone.

"Darrell? Are you okay? Can you hear me?" With the headset covering his face, she couldn't see if his eyes were open or closed. "Darrell, answer me!"

Karen had to admit she was getting scared. She knew Vinnie Pinchey would never get scared, not even a little, but then, Vinnie Pinchey would never get into a situation as bad as this. Karen decided to risk asking a neighbor. Most of the neighbors didn't know her family anyway. If she could find a good Vinnie Pinchey neighbor, that person would not gossip about what had happened here. The odds were greatly in her favor that most of her neighbors were Vinnie Pinchey. On the other hand – how many hands was that now? – a real Vinnie Pinchey neighbor would not be willing to help another neighbor. She had heard those exact words come out of the new president's mouth when he made his speech about how much better off he was since he had become the president, how much closer he was to the essence of Vinnie Pinchey as president, not having to think about others, especially poor people who always wanted more of something or other. He was so very proud to announce how now, as the nation's president, he could do whatever he wanted all the time, and he would be able to get a lot more of the things he wanted for himself: money, admiration, attention, fame.

"I'll be right back," Karen said to Darrell, hoping he could still hear her. "Wait here."

As she ran toward the back door, the ridiculousness of what she had just said hit her like a fly swatter and she began to giggle. Of course, he was going to wait there. Where could he go? He could not even move!

"Darlene!" Karen shouted, still giggling, as soon as she got in the house. "Darlene! Where are you? I really need you to come outside and help me!"

"Mom," Darlene said, in a very convincing Vinnie Pinchey manner of speaking, "I am in the middle of a very important Vinnie Pinchey meditation. This is the most important thing I have ever done in my life, and you have interrupted me. Now, right at this very moment, I must ask you to tone down your irritating voice and not speak to me, while I attempt to re-enter the positive Vinnie Pinchey state, without having to start over from the beginning. You, of all people, know I do not have any time to waste. Now, if you will kindly, or even unkindly, excuse me, I am going back right now, thank you, and goodbye."

Karen did not like her daughter to speak to her in this way, but this was not the time to deal with Darlene. After all, she was merely doing what everyone else was doing, and she was making a real effort to make a positive change in her life, a change toward the entire Vinnie Pinchey society that was coming to pass. Instead of replying to her daughter's announcement, she ran through the house and out the front door.

These days, it was easy to see which families had gone completely Vinnie Pinchey, because their houses were all the same shade of pukey green with doors the same tone of dirty red. In this neighborhood, that included all of the houses except one: the house across the street where the little girl who had been kicked out of school for being anti-Vinnie Pinchey lived. Karen looked from that house to the one beside it. Both had all the blinds closed; neither showed any sign of life within, the true essence of Vinnie Pinchey, locked up tight, resisting any kind of coalition with the neighbors. Karen could remember a time when neighbors did talk to each other, but she had always been so involved with her own life and the life of her family, when the Vinnie Pinchey attitude separated people into their own little circles, she welcomed it as a blessing. She no longer had to feel guilty for not being friendly, because nobody was friendly any more. The trait of friendliness was not expected or even accepted any more.

She decided to go with the Vinnie Pinchey family next door to the family of rebels, mainly so she would not have to explain to anyone who might see her associating with that family, and even bringing one of them over to her house. She ran up the porch, took note that all the porch furniture had been removed, as was the current trend (Vinnie Pinchey had no furniture on her front porch) and stopped herself before she began to pound on the door. She had to appear sophisticated, in control, respectable, Vinnie Pinchey. She tapped on the door in her best Vinnie Pinchey fashion.

She could hear sounds of people moving about inside the house, but no one came to answer the door. Maybe they couldn't hear her light tapping. She tapped again, a bit louder than she had before. She waited, formulating her speech in her mind. If she didn't state her case in the right Vinnie Pinchey way, she would not be able to get any help from them. Her thoughts went to her husband, and the image of him lying on the ground, helpless. She needed someone to help her, right now!

Karen tapped on the door more loudly this time, losing what little Vinnie Pinchey patience she had left. She had to get some help, and these neighbors were ignoring her! Well, again, wasn't that what Vinnie Pinchey was all about? Do whatever you want to do, and forget about the needs and desires of everyone else. It sure was so much easier when you were on the other side of Vinnie Pinchey, the side that did not need any help.

The door in front of her jerked open suddenly, and Karen's carefully crafted speech flew out of her brain. A man with an air about him that reeked Vinnie Pinchey stood there, holding the door open a few inches with his sticking-up nose poking through it. His expression said he had anything but patience for whatever reason she had disturbed his afternoon.

"I need help!" she cried, in a voice that certainly was not in any way Vinnie Pinchey. "My husband was crushed by a tree branch in our back yard and I can't lift it off of him! Please, can you help me?" She almost reached for his arm, then she stopped herself before she violated the Vinnie Pinchey code of touching – or rather, not touching anyone else. "I live right across the street, there, in that house. It will only take a minute or two." She pointed in the general direction of the house, but was unable to take her eyes off the expression of this man. Seriously, he was all Vinnie Pinchey.

"I appreciate your situation," he replied, completely in control of his voice, "and you do, indeed, have a problem you may or may not be able to solve on your own, or with help you seek from others. However, as I am sure you must be aware, good citizen as you seem to be, Vinnie Pinchey is coming on in fewer than five minutes. Therefore, I am not at liberty to leave the house, as we are in this as a family, we are gathering at this very moment around the giant screen, and our family time cannot be in any way interrupted, cut short or denied. So, there you have it, just like that.

"I thank you for your understanding of this extremely important matter. Now, I would suggest you hurry on home, back to your own house and your own family, and gather together in front of your own large screen, if you do not have a giant screen, and, by the look of your house and the cars you own, I would highly doubt that you and your family would have a giant screen on which to tune in to Vinnie Pinchey, and... where was I going with this? Oh, you stranger, you have made me lose my train of thought, so I might as well shut the door. Hurry along, so you don't miss the beginning! The beginning is always the best part of the entire program, as I am sure you must be aware, because it comes before any of the rest of the program. Thank you, and I beg for your release of this conversation. Goodbye. There is no need to bother us again, at any time."

He closed the door in her face and she could hear his frantic footsteps as he rushed to join his family in front of their giant screen.

Now Karen had a real dilemma on her hands. She knew she was expected to get home immediately so she would not miss even a second of Vinnie Pinchey, but she also was desperate to get help for her husband as soon as possible. She knew all the other neighbors would be settled down right now – no one dared miss Vinnie Pinchey and no businesses were even open while Vinnie Pinchey was being shown – should she risk going to the one other neighbor to ask for help?

FRIEND OR FOE?

When I heard rapid knocking on the front door, my first thought was of Terry. He must have been set free, and was now standing right on the porch! Zoey and I were sitting at the kitchen table playing an old-fashioned board game, something we could do without coming across anything having to do with that 'forbidden name.' It was my turn, and as I jumped up from my chair, Zoey protested.

"You have to take your turn!" she insisted. When she realized I was leaving the room and going to the door, her tone turned to panic. "Mommy, no! Don't answer it! Don't answer it! I don't want the police to take you away from me! Mommy! Please, stay here with me!"

It had not occurred to me before that the police would come to our house to arrest me; after all, what had I done besides make a few phone calls that resulted in talking to people who had gone absolutely bananas? I slowed my steps.

"It is going to be okay, Sweetie," I called to her in the most soothing voice I could muster.

The knocking on the door was sounding frantic. Deep within me, I could feel this was the sound of someone in trouble, and I could not refuse to assist anyone who needed my help. Still, I peeked through an opening in the blinds, to make sure we were going to be safe.

An enormous eye was looking right at me, another person attempting to peek inside our home.

"Ahh!" I yelled in surprise, jumping back.

"Please, help me!" a woman cried. "I need your help, right now! Please! My husband is in trouble!"

"Okay, just a second," I said through the door, as I unlocked and opened it. "Come in, come in."

She tumbled into the front room, her eyes wild, her hair all over the place. I started to close the door behind her, but she grabbed my arm.

"No, I need you to come with me," she said, panting. She did not even pause to catch her breath as she began to tell me what happened. "My husband, we live across the street, right there, in that house, the only other one that has not yet been painted that dreary green like all the other houses on this street and in this neighborhood and all over town, for that matter, even though our daughter has been insisting we paint it, and I do not like that color at all, and fortunately, my husband has not felt like painting it, so he hasn't gone to get the paint yet, and don't you think it's crazy? All this is going on, and everyone acting so foolish and every-thing, but what can you do? You have to do the best you can for your family and try to make everyone happy, and then you are not happy, so what can you do? What can you do? Oh, oh, what am I saying? I must be in shock or something. Is that a thing? Is that what is happening to me, or what else could be going on? I am going on and on, and I need to come out and say it. What am I saying? Sometimes I feel like I must be the only one going crazy, and, what, everyone else is sane? Or have I gone into another alter-nate parallel reality, where nothing makes sense to me? Because I can't understand it, do you know what I mean? I mean, your house is still a beautiful blue color, and I cannot begin to tell you how that makes me feel, what a comfort it is to me to look out and see this house across the street from ours and to not have to look at that horrible green color, and with that dirty rose trim? Who ever thought those colors would look good on a house, I mean, do you know what I mean?" She paused and was now panting even harder than she had been when she first came into the house.

"I haven't been out of the house since..." I began, but didn't want to finish the sentence. "We have been spending a lot of time at home lately, but I will agree with you. People are acting kind of strange around here."

"Around here?" she asked incredulously. Her eyes were

growing wild as she grabbed my arm and clung to me. "Around here? People are going crazy all over the city, all over the state, all over the country, all over the world! Have you not been tuning in to the current event? Buildings all over the world have already been painted that awful color! If you go to the department stores, in the clothing area, they are filled with everything that ugly green color, and all the accessories are that same dirty rose color. Oh, how I wish I had bought a few pairs of black shoes when the stores still had them in stock. And have you been to a grocery store lately? All they have on the shelves are those stupid shakes and those stupid pills and a whole bunch of vegetables, most of the kinds I have never even heard of, much less seen in the store, like the huge, enormous pile of rutabagas. I didn't even know what they were until I saw the sign. I had no idea what they even looked like until I saw them in the store."

"Rutabagas?" I asked, surprised to hear that word surfacing again. I was trying to get a picture in my mind of what was happening, not only in our community, but all over the world. She seemed to be right about one thing: people everywhere were acting strange.

"I mean, how do you even cook one of those things? And even if I did, our daughter would never even eat it." She paused and let my arm go, and her expression changed. "Oh, I am so sorry," she said, and took a step back from me. "I heard about your daughter. I am so sorry. How could this have happened to her? Isn't she only a little girl? I mean, how could a little girl like your daughter be in so much trouble at such a young age? Why didn't she go along with what they were doing in class, instead of being so rebellious? Really, she got herself in a lot of trouble by not going along with everything the teacher and the authorities were telling her to do. What are you going to do? I guess you're going to have to move to another town, since she can never go back to school in this town. Is that what you're going to do? Are you going to move to another town? Or what are you going to do? You are not qualified to teach your own child all the way through school, are you? Or, are you? You don't look like a teacher."

"No, I am not a teacher, and, by the way, who are you, anyway?"

I asked. I did not like the idea of someone else coming into my house, especially someone I had never even met before today, and telling me what I was not qualified to do.

"Oh, I am so sorry, I forgot to introduce myself! I'm Karen, from across the street, oh I already said that, right in the house right there, the house that is not painted that ugly color of green with the dirty reddish trim. Oh, I already said that, too, didn't I? So, I live right there with my husband and my daughter. My husband's name is Darrell, and my daughter is Darlene, she is 14 and she goes to the high school now. She is the one who told me about your daughter. I guess it's common knowledge all over town by now, about your daughter being kicked out of school, I mean. Oh! Oh, my! I forgot why I even came over here! I need your help! My husband! Darrell! I need you to come with me! I need help! I can't move the branch by myself!"

"What are you talking about? What branch?" I was beginning to think she was another crazy one around here.

"My husband, Darrell, oh, I already told you his name, was in the back yard, and I don't know what happened, but my daughter and I were in the house, and we heard this loud crash in the back yard, and we looked out and we saw this giant branch from the tree had fallen right on my husband, Darrell. So, I went out to help him, but I am not strong enough to lift the branch off of him by myself. So, I went to your next-door neighbors, right there over on that side, but they couldn't help me, they were too busy with the family thing and the program was coming on right at that exact time. So, I came over here to ask if you or your husband or maybe both of you can come over across the street with me, and help me lift the branch off of my husband, Darrell."

Apparently, she hadn't heard about my husband being arrested, although it obviously was common knowledge about what had happened to Zoey. Also, what about Zoey? I couldn't leave her in the house by herself.

"My husband isn't home right now, but I can come and help you. Maybe together we can move the branch. Zoey, come on in here. We need to go across the street with – what did you say your name is? Karen?"

"Do you have to bring her? Can she stay here? It will only take a few minutes," Karen urged.

"No, she can't stay at home by herself. It's okay, she won't be in the way."

"Well, okay, we better get going," she said, moving toward the door. "I probably left Darrell lying there alone too long. I hope he is still conscious."

"Come on, Zoey, let's go with Karen to her house." Zoey hesitantly came out of the kitchen and ran over to me and clamped onto my hand. I grabbed my keys and locked the door on the way out. The three of us dashed across the deserted street to Karen's house.

We ran up onto her porch, and she reached for the doorknob, slamming herself into the door. "I know I didn't lock it!" she exclaimed. She began pounding on the door with her fist.

"Darlene! Open the door! It's me, Mom! Come on! Open the door!" When her daughter didn't respond, Karen grew panicky. "Open the door! I didn't bring my keys! Why did you lock it? Darlene! Darlene! Open the door! Do you hear me? I said, 'open the door!' Right now!"

"Is there another way to get into your back yard?" I asked. Maybe we can go through the gate or something?"

"No, I don't have the key to the gate, and besides, it doesn't open from the outside."

"Can we climb over the fence? Or maybe we can go through the neighbor's yard and get in from there?"

"No, the fence is too high. And we don't even know the neighbors, but the fence is even higher all around the back yard. Darlene! Open the door!" Karen pounded on the door nonstop for a few minutes, while continuing to yell to her daughter. Zoey clung tightly to my hand, watching me with great fear in her eyes. I smiled at her to reassure her, but she wouldn't smile back at me.

Suddenly, the air was pierced with a screeching sound that

was coming closer and closer to us. A man was running down middle of the street and he was screaming. As he got closer, I could see he was wearing only a towel around his waist. He was barefoot, and charging down the street as if he were being chased by wild tigers. He ran past the house, still screaming, around the corner and out of sight. A couple of seconds later, two gigantic dogs, possibly a mix between Doberman and Great Dane, came charging down the street and followed him around the corner. I squatted down and pulled Zoey's face into my chest, so she did not have to look at this strange and disturbing sight.

Karen kept pounding on the door. Finally, after what seemed hours, but was probably about ten minutes, we could hear the sound of the door being unlocked. Karen opened the door and we went inside the house. Her daughter was not in sight.

"Come on, we can get to the back yard through the kitchen," Karen said, motioning us for her to follow her.

When we got to the kitchen our path to the back door was blocked by Karen's daughter. She stood there with her arms crossed, legs apart, and she had a very angry look on her face.

"What is SHE doing here?" Darlene demanded. "Get her out of my house immediately! She is not welcome here, she has no business here, in my house, so get her out of here right now, and I mean immediately, and even sooner than that!"

It took me a moment to realize she was talking about Zoey. At first, I thought she meant me, but she was looking at Zoey with the meanest look in her eyes I have ever seen. Zoey began to cry.

"Darlene!" Karen shouted. "Our neighbors are here to help Dad's situation in the back yard. Come on, you can help us too. We have to get the branch off of Dad."

"I already told you, Mother, and I am positive you were listening to me then, so you better listen to me now, and if you were listening or were not listening then, listen to me now: I don't feel like going outside right now, and you can't make me. It was bad enough you interrupted the program with your pounding on the door. You could have waited until the program was over. Why did you have to try to interrupt the most important program in the world? You are pushing it, you know. If you don't get with the program right away, our family is going to be an outcast family like the one you brought here now. So, get them out of our house, right now. This is not what I want. I do not want these people, this kind of people, in my house. How dare you bring them into my house, and especially at a time like this? These are not the kind of people we should have in our house at any time, and especially not as a time such as this. Get them out of here right now, Mother, and I mean it!"

"Darlene, do you think you are being a little bit overdramatic?" Karen asked. "They are here to help me, because you are refusing to help me. And I do not like your tone of voice, young lady."

"I think we'd better go," I said, not wanting to be the center of attention, nor wanting to continue to expose Zoey to such hatred and rudeness. I grabbed Zoey and pulled her close to me, in an effort to protect her from this awful manner of speaking.

"You can't talk to me like that, Mother, because I am doing everything in the correct and proper fashion. You did not see today's training lesson, so you don't know how I am to behave, or am not to behave. You would have greatly benefited from watching the program with me, but you had to go off and do your own kind of thing that had nothing to do with the program. You better watch out, Mother, or you will be just like our neighbors, and everyone will despise you too."

"Darlene!" Karen stopped and took a deep breath. "I am asking you very kindly, please step out of the way, so our nice neighbor can go with me to the back yard and help me get the big branch off of your dad. I am not raising my voice to you, because I know that is not proper, but I am asking you, no, I am insisting that you move out of the way so we can go about our business that has nothing to do with you and your attitude right now."

"Mother! You have a lot to learn. I recorded today's program, and you better go in and watch it right now, before you do any kind of damage to our family."

"Darlene, I have something more important to do right now, and that is to rescue your father. Don't you care that he is lying on the ground in the back yard, being crushed by a huge tree branch? I can watch the program later. No, I promise I will watch the program later, but right now I have to do this. I am asking you kindly to please step out of the way so we may pass by you. If you insist our neighbors go home, I will insist you go outside with me and help me move the tree branch."

"Mother, you are making it very difficult for us to live in the ideal household."

"Darlene, with your father lying in the back yard under a tree branch, this is pretty far from the ideal household. I am telling you that right now."

Darlene stomped her foot and rolled her eyes, looking at the ceiling. "Oh, alright, I will let you guys go to the back yard, but, Mother, you better not let anyone know, ever, that these outcasts were anywhere near our house." She stepped to the side and let us walk by her. I continued to hold Zoey close to me.

When we finally made it to the back yard, I was shocked to see the extent of the damage. A huge branch still connected to an enormous tree was lying across the yard, filling up almost the entire back yard. I couldn't see Karen's husband anywhere. I did see some weird kind of sword lying on the ground over on one side of the yard.

"He is right over there," Karen said, making her way between the smaller branches of the tree that were spread all over the yard. "I'm coming, Honey," she called to her husband.

I stayed as close as I could to her, and finally I was able to see a man on the ground. He had some weird kind of helmet on his head. He was lying perfectly still, and I wondered if he were breathing. The branch was crushing his chest.

"Darrell? Darrell? Can you hear me? I am back, and I have brought help with me. We are going to lift this branch off of you, and everything is going to be fine."

She motioned for me to move over to one side of the huge branch, and she grabbed the other side. I set Zoey in one of the few open areas in the yard, away from the large branch.

"So, where are we going with this branch?" I asked. "Since it is still attached to the tree, we are not going to be able to move it very far."

"Oh, we don't have to move it very far, we just have to lift it up off of him. Then he will be able to get up and move out from underneath it." She seemed very satisfied with her answer, but I was not.

"Is he going to be able to move by himself? Is he even conscious? He isn't moving at all."

"Oh, he's okay, he's fine. He's just not talking right now. Maybe he's embarrassed because you are here, and he doesn't want anyone to see him in this position. If I were in his place, I wouldn't want anyone to see me. Would you? I mean, if you were in a situation like this, would you want other people to see you?"

"To be honest, I can't even see him, because he has that mask on his face. But I think you should get some kind of a reaction out of him before we attempt to lift this branch off of him, so he can move."

"Darrell, Sweetie, can you say something so we know you are okay? We want to lift this branch up off you, and then you can move out from under it. Will you be able to do that?" She looked at me. "He's a fireman. He should be able to do nearly anything."

"It is a pretty large branch," I said, "and I'm not sure you and I can lift it ourselves."

"Sure, we can! We are a lot stronger than we think we are. You know that slogan, don't you?"

"Actually, I don't know the slogan, but just because it is a slogan it doesn't mean it is true."

"Well, I hate to say it, but it does seem like this rutabaga didn't fall far from the tree. Now I see you where she gets it. Is her father like this, too? Or only you? I guess it takes only one. But it's too bad she didn't go the other way."

"I have no idea what you're talking about, but are we going to do this or not? I have other things I need to do, and I can't stand here all day discussing rutabagas." Actually, I didn't have much else to do, but I did want to get Zoey out of this wacky environment, and myself as well.

"Okay, when I count to fourteen, then we will both lift together, on my count. Are you ready?"

"Why are you going to count all the way to fourteen? How about something simpler, like three?"

"Just three? Will three be enough?" She looked very puzzled.

"Yes! Three will be enough! You don't have to count all the way to fourteen!"

"Really? I'm not sure if I should listen to you right now, because, what do you know, anyway?"

"Look, do you want my help or not? If you want me to help, let's do this now." I was thinking, if she had already started counting, she would be to fourteen by now.

"Okay, we are in this together. One, two, three, four, five, six, seven, eight—"

"Mother!" Darlene shouted out the back window. "Mother, you have to get these people out of our yard right now. You are taking way too long, and how does that look? I really don't care what you have to do, but they need to leave right now."

"Darlene, if they leave right now, then I need you to come back here and help me. I already told you, I can't do this by myself. The branch is too heavy."

"Well, you better hurry up! You have no idea what this is doing to me, to our family, to our entire reputation."

"Okay," Karen said to me, "where was I?"

"You were on eight," I said.

"Did I already say 'eight?' Or was I about to say 'eight?'"

"You already said 'eight,'" I said.

Zoey's little voice chimed in. "Doesn't this lady know how to count, Mommy?"

"Zoey, Sweetie, be quiet and let the adults do the talking right now."

"Okay, Mommy. I love you!"

"Why did she say that?" Karen asked.

"You just said 'eight,'" I reminded her.

"Oh, yes, I guess I can keep counting from there. Here we go again. Nine, ten, eleven, twelve, thirteen, fourteen!"

I lifted with all my strength, but the branch didn't budge.

"Oh, I forgot to lift," Karen said apologetically. "Okay, let's start over again. Ready? On the count of fourteen."

"How about if we just both lift it now?" I suggested.

"Hey, not a bad idea," Karen said. "Okay, ready, lift!"

We both lifted at the same time, as was previously planned, and the branch was raised a tiny bit off Karen's husband.

"We did it!" she shouted. "We did it! See? I told you we could do it. You didn't believe me, but we did it!"

We were standing there with the branch an inch or so above her husband. I was unable to say a word, as all my strength was concentrated toward this one effort. I wanted to ask her what we should do now, since our hands were full of a tree branch, and her husband wasn't moving. At that moment, she used her foot to shove her husband over to one side, as the branch slipped out of my hands and fell to the ground, barely missing him. I fell backwards, fortunately, onto another branch laying on the ground, and it broke my fall.

"Mommy!" Zoey shouted. "Are you okay? Did you get hurt?"

My heart was pounding, but I was able to speak now.

"I'm okay," I called to her.

I looked over the branch and saw Karen leaning over her husband.

"Darrell? Darrell? Darrell, answer me!"

I was beginning to have my doubts as to whether he was still alive.

"Darrell, I don't care if you can hear me or not, but I need you to answer me, or move, or do something to let me know you are okay. Otherwise, I am going to have to call emergency services to come and check on you. You don't want to go to the hospital, do you? That would not be at all Vinnie Pinchey."

There was that expression again. Now the entire attitude of this family was beginning to make sense to me. I shot a glanced at Zoey, and the pained look on her face told me she had heard the expression, too.

"We need to go now," I said, pulling myself up out of the tree branch and scraping the yard debris from my clothes.

"No!" Karen said. "I need you to help me get my husband inside the house."

"If he can't make it into the house on his own, I think you need to call emergency services." I was not about to suggest that she call the morgue. I was going to let her figure that out on her own. I doubted calling the morgue would be very Vinnie Pinchey, and wasn't that the most important thing to everyone else these days?

"Come on, Darrell, you need to get yourself up, because the neighbors aren't helping us anymore."

I heard a slight moan coming from Darrell. "Take. This. Thing. Off. My. Head."

"Do you want me to remove your virtual reality helmet?" Karen asked with the sound of surprise in her voice.

"Take. It. Off. Now."

Well, he was sounding pretty good to me now. At least he was speaking, and that told me a lot about his vital signs.

"Zoey, let's go now. Karen, you've got this. You can get him into the house."

I walked over to Zoey and grabbed her hand. As we approached the kitchen door to through the house and get back home,

Darlene was standing there, once again blocking our way.

"I am saying this in the most calm and delicate way, you two are not going to walk into this house again." She stuck her nose up in the air as she spoke. "You are not welcome here, and you have no reason to come here now or at any time in the future, and especially right now. So, you can just go to your own house and I would be extremely satisfied if you would never even look in the direction of our house again."

"I am saying this in the most calm and delicate way, my daughter and I need to walk through your house in order to get to our house. We don't want to look at anything in your house, or touch anything in your house, or spend any time inside your house. We want to go home, and this is the only way we can get from here to there," I stated, calmly and with much respect.

"Mother, will you please tell your unwelcome visitors they are not allowed inside our house? We have heard all about you, and we know your beliefs are very different from ours, because of your rebellious and ridiculous actions. As a matter of fact, we don't even let our other neighbors inside our house, the ones who do share our beliefs, so why would we let you and your outcast family into our house, ever? I do believe I should call the authorities right now, and have them pick you up, and take you and lock you up, forever. That way your antisocial and rebellious attitudes would not be able to spread to anyone else. Really, I think that is a very good idea. None of us want you living in our neighborhood, on our street. We don't want your kind associating with us anytime, anywhere, in any fashion."

Zoey started crying again. She was saying something, but I couldn't understand her crying language.

"Oh, that's just great. Use a crybaby to try to get your own way," Darlene said. "It is not going to work, I can tell you that right here and now."

"Can someone give me a hand here?" Karen shouted from across the yard. "I could use a little help. Either one of you, I need a little help."

"Mother, can't you see you I am busy right now? I already

told you, I don't want to go outside right now. You can't make me do anything I don't want to do. If you were watching the program today like you should have been, like every good law-abiding citizen was doing, instead of running around the neighborhood and trying to make friends with these outcasts, you would be fully aware of that principle."

"If you will excuse me," I said, trying to push my way past Darlene, "we will be going home now."

She continued to block the doorway. "I don't want to move, and I don't have to do anything I don't want to do. That is the freedom of our society. That is one of our rights, and you can't take it away from me. An outcast like you can't make me do anything I don't want to do."

I decided to play along. "Okay, Darlene, if you do not want to let us go through your house, we will have to stay here, right here in your back yard, forever, I guess."

"Mommy," Zoey cried, "I don't want to stay here forever."

"Well, Zoey, I guess we don't have any choice. Miss Darlene will not let us walk through her house, and we don't have any other way to get to our house from here."

"How dare you call me Miss Darlene! And you are correct. I will not let you walk through our house ever again, because I don't want any of your outcast attitude rubbing off on our furniture, or seeping into our air. I know who you are, and I know exactly what you are trying to do, and you can be warned right now, here and now, I want this to be known and stated, right now, at this very time, and at no other, not earlier at another time, not later at another time, but right here and now while I have your undivided attention, I know what you are trying to do, and you are not going to get away with it."

"Mommy, would this be a good time for us to say a prayer?" Zoey asked. "Daddy always says we should pray when we don't know what to do, and I don't know what to do now."

"Zoey, you can pray inside your head, please, but not out loud right now," I told her.

"Can someone please give me a hand?" Karen asked. "It will only take a minute. Come on, either of you, or even better, both of you?" I looked back and saw she had her husband propped up on the ground beside her, and she was trying to lift him to his feet.

"I already told you, Mother, I don't feel like coming outside right now. When are you going to get that through your walnut-shaped head, anyway? Besides, I am busy protecting my house, and this is the most important thing I have ever done in my life," Darlene said, in an extremely rude fashion.

I was frustrated. I needed to get out of this yard, Karen needed help, and our efforts were being blocked by this bratty teenager.

Meanwhile, in Another County

Terry was worried sick about his family. He had not been allowed to contact them, and he didn't know if they were safe. He had tried to get permission send a message to his wife but the effort was not successful. At this point, he didn't know where he was or how long he had been here. After he was arrested, he had been transported in the middle of the night from the county jail to some other prison, where he had been held in solitary confinement ever since. He had not had the chance to speak to a lawyer, go to court, go before a judge, or even speak to anyone besides the prison guards who brought his food, a pile of overcooked, unflavored, unrecognizable substance, possibly some kind of blended vegetables. Contrary to popular belief, he was not let out of solitary confinement for one hour per day.

Terry still didn't understand why he had been brought to this place, or why he had been arrested in the first place. He had never broken a law or a rule in his entire life. That one day – he wasn't sure how long ago it had been, since he was in total darkness all the time and had no concept of day or night – he went to the school to pick up his daughter after he had been called, and the next thing he knew, he was being thrown in the back of a police car. He knew this whole thing had to be illegal and against his constitutional rights, but if nobody knew he were here, these guys who were in charge – were they even the police? – could do just about anything to him and nobody would ever know.

He heard the rattling of metal wheels coming down the hall, signaling it was again mealtime. He had to get an answer from the guard. He had to communicate with his wife.

Reasoning with the guards was not an option, because they were completely unreasonable. Still, he had to try again. When he heard the cart getting close to his cell door, he called out to the guard.

"Hello? Is anybody out there? I need to talk to somebody. I think I'm getting sick. As a matter of fact, I am very sick. Can you send in a doctor? Or can you take me to the infirmary?"

"You better watch it, Buster, or I am going to let you out of there. And if you get in with the general population, do you know what they are going to do to you? I have a feeling they will tear you limb from limb. Even the rest of the prisoners don't have any sympathy for your kind. Not only are you not fit to be a part of society, you are not fit to be part of prison society. I don't know why I am even bothering to talk to you, because it is obvious you have no morals, no scruples, and no common sense. You are another wacko case, and you need to stay locked away until the day you rot to death in here. And then, you can just rot in hell for the rest of eternity."

He slammed the plate through the small opening and laughed gleefully.

"Technically," Terry shouted through the steel door, "a person will not rot in hell. He will burn in hell. Haven't you ever read the Bible?"

"Oh, you think you're so smart because you know stuff," the guard replied with a sneer in his voice. "Everyone knows that you don't have to know stuff to be smart. And especially you, Buster, you better watch it and you don't try to play smart perks with me. Why would anyone, ever, in their right mind bother to read any book, much less the Bible, when we can learn everything we need to know about everything relevant to our lives by watching Vinnie Pinchey? Oh, I forgot! You are not in your right mind! Ha-ha-ha-ha-ha-ha!

"By the way, how do you like your rutabagas?" He stomped down the hall chuckling to himself.

Terry was more frustrated than ever now. What could he do? How could he get out of here? How could he get any help? How could he get any answers? He had been praying the whole time he was here, and he knew he was not out of God's sight; and he knew God had not forgotten about him.

And he knew his patience and his help were coming from the Lord. He also knew he held onto his sanity only because of the power of God inside him.

Across Town

Michael was very upset about the sequence of events that had been happening in his town. First, Terry stopped showing up for work, had not called in to say he would not be there, and Michael had no idea why. Terry had never missed a day of work in his entire life. He had never called in sick, so this was extremely unusual for him. He had tried calling Terry's cell phone, but a very strange person had answered and given Michael some wacky kind of answer and refused to put Terry on the line. Michael had driven by Terry's house several times, but when he saw his car was not there, he knew Terry would not be at home either. He had tried calling Terry's wife on the home phone number, but every time he called, the line was either busy or gave a message that this number could not be reached at this time. Since more than week had passed since Terry's disappearance, Michael decided to call the police.

"Hello, I would like to report a missing person," he began.

"I know who you are, and I know exactly what you are trying to do, and you can be warned right now, here and now, I want this to be known and stated, right now, at this very time, and at no other, not earlier at another time, not later at another time, but right here and now while I have your undivided attention, that I know what you are trying to do, and you are not going to get away with it. It is being broadcast at this very moment, at this exact time, and everyone knows what you are trying to do, and how you are at the root of the dissatisfaction, and, frankly, we are not going to tolerate it. As a matter of fact, and you can take note of this, Mr. Huffy-Puffy, if I were you, I would move myself and my pitiful thing you call a family to the farthest available uninhabitable planet, so as to no longer inflict such pain on the rest of our smooth-functioning society."

"What? What are you saying? What are you talking about? I am trying to report a missing person."

"You are not the person who is eligible or even permitted to report a missing person, and if you call this number again, if you EVER call this number EVER again, I am telling you right here and now, you are going to regret it for the rest of your life."

"What? Who are you? Are you threatening me?"

"Don't you try to play smart perks with me, Mr. Huffy-Puffy! And you should know better than to call at this time, at this very time, when it is only five minutes or fewer for the program to resume! You better get in front of your large screen, or your giant screen, and get with the program before you throw it all away. Then you'll be sorry! Then you will very definitely be sorry! Goodbye, and do not bother to call this number ever again, especially if you are having an emergency. We do not like your type, and we do not have time nor space for you in our agenda!"

The phone on the other end was slammed down, somewhat hurting Michael's ear. Michael was stunned. This conversation had so confused him, he didn't know even what to think. He was a logical man, an engineer, and he expected everything, including words in conversations, to be placed in a logical manner that made sense to him. What this person had just told him made no sense at all.

"Mickey!" he called to his ten-year-old daughter, who was upstairs studying. "Mickey, come on down here!"

"Yes, Daddy?" she said, a tinge of worry in her voice. "Is everything okay?" She came padding down the steps quickly to see what he wanted.

"Yes, Sweetheart," Michael said, upset with himself for causing her any worry. Since his wife had passed away two years ago, he had become very protective of his daughter. They had bonded closely during the heart-breaking months when her mother was in the hospital dying. Every day, he thanked God for his daughter, who looked so much like a little replica of her mother, it broke his heart. He was so very thankful to have a part of his wife still alive and right here with him. "Everything is fine. I want to go for a drive, over to Terry's house, and I want you to ride along with me."

"Okay, Daddy, let me get my sweater." She skipped up the steps while Michael collected his keys and wallet from their cubbyhole in his little home office. She returned to the living room at the same time he did, and they went out to the garage together.

"Is everything okay with Terry?" Mickey asked, as they fastened their seat belts in Michael's new electric car. He pushed the car's start button and pressed the switch to open the garage door, checking to be sure the car battery was sufficiently charged.

"Why do you ask that?" Michael asked, slightly distracted, as he ran down the list of instrument indicators on the panel.

"For one thing, we have not ever gone over to his house before," she said. "What's the matter? Is he sick or something?"

Everything looked good on the instrument panel, and the battery had plenty of charge, so he backed out of the garage and closed the garage door, waiting to make sure it was fully closed, as he always did, before proceeding down the street.

"Since we have not ever gone to his house, I think this would be a good time to go over there, right now. Don't you?" He smiled at his daughter, then returned his focus to the road.

"Yes, Daddy, I think it is a good idea. He has a daughter, right?"

"Yes, her name is Zoey, and I think she is about six or seven years old."

Mickey was a bit disappointed that she wasn't closer to her own age, but she knew she could be friends with anybody. She was looking forward to meeting another little girl, especially one whose dad worked with her dad. Their dads had worked together for more than five years, and this would be the first time the daughters would meet. She smiled at the thought of a new little friend.

"I already know I am going to like her," she told her dad, feeling a smile all inside of her.

Nick and Company

"Samia, it is your turn to put the dishes in the dishwasher," Sharia said, as soon as they sat down at the dinner table.

"I don't have to if I don't want to," Samia said defiantly. "Or were you not paying attention to Vinnie Pinchey today? She said you can't tell me what to do."

"But it's your turn! I did it last night!"

"That is at least seven minutes I could be spending doing my own thing, and Vinnie Pinchey would definitely approve of me doing my own thing," Samia said, holding her nose high in the air, in her best Vinnie Pinchey style.

"Seven minutes? It takes you seven minutes to put the dishes in the dishwasher? I can do it in four."

"You cannot!"

"I can so! I set the timer every night when it's my turn, and I am down to four minutes now."

"You are a dreamer, Sis, if you think you can do it in four minutes."

"I am indeed no dreamer, I'm just such a fast worker. I don't waste any time when I have work to do."

"And that is my point exactly. I do not want to have to do any work."

The girls were so caught up in their argument they hadn't noticed there was no food cooking on the stove. Nothing had been prepared for their dinner and their mother was not in the kitchen. They had been so well trained to be at the table at six o'clock sharp, they never thought to question whether or not any food would be ready for them.

"So, you are, like, telling Mom she has to put the dishes in the dishwasher?" Sharia asked.

"I never said that," Samia said, staring up at the ceiling. "I don't care who does it. I am just saying I don't feel like doing it, so I don't have to do it. You heard Vinnie Pinchey. We can do whatever we want, all the time. I wonder when Dad is going to paint the kitchen? It is so NOT Vinnie Pinchey with this color, and especially the wallpaper on that one wall. I am so glad none of our friends ever see our kitchen!"

"Yeah, me too," Sharia agreed. "I am never going to invite anyone I know over here until our house is all Vinnie Pinchey and all my clothes are Vinnie Pinchey and our whole family is completely Vinnie Pinchey."

"I know Mom and Dad are trying, but, really, if you have to TRY to be Vinnie Pinchey, ARE you really Vinnie Pinchey?"

"They are doing their best! But, yeah, I see your point. We have to give them some credit, though, and if they can do their best to fake it, we will be okay. Our family will not be judged harshly if they are trying their best."

"Do you hear someone screaming outside?" Samia asked.

"I don't know. Maybe," Sharia shrugged. "What difference does it make? It doesn't matter one tiny bit to us. What would Vinnie Pinchey do?"

"Vinnie Pinchey would not be wasting her thoughts, her words, or her precious moments on this topic, I can tell you that one thing for sure!" Samia announced, proud to be so Vinnie Pinchey, and at the same time trying to ignore the screaming going on outside the house.

"I wonder where Mom and Dad are?" Sharia asked, after a few seconds of relative silence. "What could they be doing to make them late for dinner? They have never been late for dinner before. Don't you think it is rather unusual?"

"Another topic for us to not be wasting our thoughts, our words, or our precious moments, my dear sister," Samia said smugly, leaning back in her chair.

Nicole drifted into the kitchen, barely aware of her daughters sitting at the table as she kept her focus on the mobile device in her hands. She was so close to making the next level, beads of sweat were popping out on her forehead. She moved over to lean against the counter so she could make the fantastic finish and enjoy the screen gems that would glisten to signal her accomplishment.

"Mom, what are we having for dinner?" Sharia asked.

"I don't know, what are we having for dinner?" Nicole asked in reply, not taking her eyes off her mobile screen.

"That's what I am asking you!" Sharia said, raising her voice.

"Your tone of voice does not sound at all Vinnie Pinchey, Sharia," her mother said. "Yes! Yes! I did it! I finally did it!" She did a little dance around the kitchen, a waltz with her mobile device, as she enjoyed the explosion of color and dazzling patterns she had earned over the past few days with her persistence, increased skill and hard work. "I did it! I did it! I knew I... could do it!" she chanted as she danced.

"Mother, I am asking you in a most calm and civilized way, what did you fix us for dinner?" Samia asked, pointing her nose high in the air.

"And I am replying to your question in a most calm and civilized way, I did not make any dinner tonight."

"But you always make dinner!" Samia cried.

"Why, Mom? You make dinner for us every night!"

"And that is my point, at this moment," Nicole replied. "I did not feel like making dinner today. Why must I make dinner every night? If I don't feel like making dinner, I don't have to make dinner. Did we not learn that exact lesson today, together, as a family?"

"We did," Samia agreed.

"So, what are we going to eat?" Sharia asked, a bit of a whine in her voice.

"Do I detect a tone of discontent in your voice, Sharia?" her mother asked.

"Yeah, Vinnie Pinchey never shows her discontent, Shar," Samia said. "You better watch out before you fall off the sky-scraper."

"I am not anywhere near the edge of the skyscraper, and you know that! I am just hungry, and I don't know what we are going to eat!"

"You are a big girl, and we have lots of food in this house. You can find something," Nicole said. She was contemplating whether or not to start on the next challenge. She was feeling a bit hungry, but then again, if she skipped dinner and kept working on this challenge all evening, she might be able to make it to the next level in a couple of days. That would give her dual satisfaction, for it would also bring her closer to her Vinnie Pinchey weight goal.

"I want you to fix it for us!" Sharia begged. "What is Dad going to eat? He is not going to want to fix his own dinner. Where is he, anyway?"

"Your dad is exactly where he wants to be, right at this very moment," Nicole said, as she mentally prepared herself to begin her next challenge.

"Where?" Samia asked. "Where is he?"

"Actually, I do not know where he is, and I am very happy he is very happy."

"Is he leaving the family?" Sharia asked, ready to dramatize every situation.

"No, he is not leaving the family," her mother assured her. "THAT would not be Vinnie Pinchey, as you are well aware."

"Please, will you fix some dinner for us?" Sharia asked again, secretly hoping, against all the new cultural values, that her mother would remain more like herself and less Vinnie Pinchey.

"No, I don't feel like it. So, there you have it, just like that," Nicole answered, and with that, she pressed 'start' and left the room, her mobile device in hand, all fired up for the next round.

Is Anybody Home?

Michael pulled his car into Terry's driveway, noting Terry's car still was absent.

"Is anybody at home?" Mickey asked him, as they got out of the car.

"I don't see Terry's car, but his wife's car is probably in the garage. I guess there is only one way to find out," Michael replied.

They climbed the steps to the porch and Michael knocked on the door. All the blinds were closed so they couldn't see inside the house.

"Can I ring the doorbell?" Mickey asked.

"Sure, go ahead."

Mickey rang doorbell twice, and stood there, waiting. "Maybe they are not home," she said.

Michael had a feeling something was wrong, and he wondered if Terry had gone to the hospital. "I am going to leave a note, so he will know we were here."

He returned to the car for his pen and pad of paper, and scribbled a note to Terry and his wife. He went back to the porch and searched for place to put it, where he was sure it would be seen. If he left it somewhere on the porch and they came into through garage, they wouldn't notice the note. He tried to see how he could fasten it to the screen door, so when they opened the door they would see it there.

While he was trying to find a place where the note would stay without falling, he heard loud yelling and screaming coming from across the street. Michael and Mickey looked in that direction, but they didn't see anyone.

"What is going on, Daddy?"

"I have no idea," Michael said, "but it sounds like somebody is in trouble."

They went to the edge of the porch and listened.

They heard voices and could catch bits of conversation, such as, "You get out of here and never come back;" "I really need help right now;" and, "Let us go! Let us go!"

"It sounds like someone needs help," Michael said. "You stay here while I go over and check it out."

"Daddy, don't leave here by myself. I'll come with you."

"No, you better wait in the car."

"But Daddy, I can help too," Mickey said.

"No, you go wait for me in the car. I will be right back. Come on, be a good girl for Daddy."

Mickey slowly walked to the car, watching as her dad sprinted across the street.

As Michael approached the house across the street, he could hear the yelling and screaming was coming from behind the house. It sounded like somebody was being held against his will. Michael ran around the house and was faced with an 8-foot fence, a solid fence, so he could not see what was happening in the back yard.

He could hear the voices more clearly now, including the sound of a child crying.

"I told you, you are not setting foot in this house ever again. We do not allow outcasts in our house."

"We don't want to set foot in your house, we only need to go through it so we can get home."

Michael thought he recognized Terry's wife's voice.

"Will somebody please help me? I really need help!" a different female voice shouted. "I can't move him all by myself."

"You guys are making too much noise, and you are taking up too much of my time!"

Michael heard a door slam.

"Now what are we going to do?"

"Hey! Do you need help back there?" Michael called. "If you open this gate, I can help."

"What is going on over there?" a man yelled from the house next door. "You are making entirely too much noise, and we can't even hear ourselves think over here. I am going to call the authorities right now."

"Is someone in trouble back there?" Michael shouted.

"Yes! I need help with my husband! I can't move him by myself!"

"Be quiet! Be quiet!"

"Get us out of here!"

"I am asking you calmly and with much respect to please be quiet and stop disturbing our peace," the neighbor said.

"Please, help us! We can't get out of this back yard!"

"If you open the gate, I can help you," Michael said again, curious as to what was happening on the other side of the fence.

"The gate is locked and we don't have the key!"

"Okay, you leave me no choice, I am calling the authorities and they will be here before you know it, and you will all be under arrest for disturbing my peace," the neighbor yelled out his window.

AT THE COUNTRY CLUB

Nick was exhausted, and in a very good way. He had been running all over the golf course for the past three hours, wearing his virtual reality glasses, on the search for his Vinnie Pinchey hidden treasures. He had found nearly all of them: only two more remained on this golf course. He had covered the entire area, so he didn't know where the last two could be. He paid 400 credits to get another clue.

"The way is true; the water is blue. What you will find will blow your mind."

The clue had to be referring to one of the four ponds on the golf course, the only places around here with blue water. He had already searched near the ponds, but he hadn't looked in the ponds. He needed to find these last two treasures, and now he was pretty sure at least one of them was in a pond. He glanced at his watch and saw it was way past dinnertime at his house, yet that didn't matter anymore. Yes, his family was very important to him, but what was more important in days such as these, he was doing exactly what he wanted to do. He really wanted to get these last two treasures while he was here at the golf course. If he had to come back another day, he would lose five of the treasures he had already accomplished.

He ran over to the nearest pond, breathing heavily. He was surprised at how few people were on the golf course today. Nobody played golf anymore, but everybody was in search of the hidden treasures which could only be seen with the Vinnie Pinchey glasses.

He stopped at the edge of the pond and began to search the top of the water with his glasses still in place. He didn't see anything, any treasures, nor any hints or clues to where a treasure may be.

He lifted glasses for moment, to see where the other people were on the golf course. Although everybody's game was different, and they would not find the hidden treasures in the same place, maybe some were bunched together, or near each other. He noticed three men were near the farthest pond, so maybe where his treasure was over there. He took one more look at this smaller pond, scanning every inch of the top of it to be sure he had not overlooked a treasure.

When he was satisfied there were no treasures in this pond, he began to jog to the farthest pond.

"Hey!" he yelled to the men near the pond. "Are you guys finding any of your treasures in this area?"

"No, but we saw a flamingo," one of the men said. They were standing together, staring at the pond.

"Is that the badge for level five?" Nick asked, walking over closer to them. "I thought it was a porcupine, but I'm only on level three right now. I probably wouldn't be able to see it yet, would I? I would have to be on level five to see it."

"No, we saw a real pink flamingo, a bird. It was right over there, standing at the end of the pond, in the water. But it flew away when we got close to it."

"What are you talking about? You saw a real, live bird?" He could not understand the importance of their statement. "Are you saying you saw a live flamingo around here? How can you get any points for that?"

"Well, it's true, you don't get any points for seeing a real pink flamingo, but it did look pretty cool."

"Did you at least take a picture of it?" Nick asked. "You might be able to get points if you upload it."

"See, I told you!" one man said to the other two.

"You didn't say anything about taking a picture."

"Well, I thought about it. I mean, I was thinking about it. I mean, I wish I would've thought about it."

"Yeah? Why didn't we think of that? We probably could've gotten a lot of points!"

"So, what level are you guys on?" Nick asked. "I only need two more before I can qualify to get the bonus points for level three. I am so excited to get to the end of this round and make it to the magic carpet ride." He had been thinking a lot about the promised magic carpet ride, and he was going to get it very soon!

"We are only on level one," the shortest man said. They looked at each other sheepishly.

"Then what are you doing here?" Nick asked. "You know the hidden treasures from levels one and two are not located here at the golf course. That is common knowledge. You do know that, don't you?"

The men looked at each other and then looked at Nick without saying anything.

"You didn't know that? You are not going to find anything on this golf course until you get to level three. I guess you have not been paying attention to the instructions."

"Well, we saw lots of men over here playing the game, so we thought we could find some of the hidden treasures here. They looked like they were finding them all over the place."

"Do you guys even know the rules and the graduated steps? You have to start in your own house. All of the hidden treasures of level one you will find in your own house. Then when you get past level one, and you have all the treasures of the bonus points, you move into your own yard. As soon as you finish your own yard, the bonus points will be somewhere in your own neighborhood, but they are usually near your own house, so you don't have to bother any of your neighbors.

"Wait a minute," he said, beginning to get angry at them. "You said 'playing the game.' We are not only playing a game here! This is serious business! I bet you guys haven't even registered yet, have you? You are trying to horn in without paying your dues. I am going to have to report you. Although it is not what I want to do, and my main goal is to focus on doing only what I want to do,

I am going to have to report you. You can't be standing around here without having paid the registration fee and acting like you are working your way up to level three."

The men looked at each other again.

"Oh, come on, you're not going to turn us in, are you? Be a buddy, and we will go. We promise you, we won't ever do it again."

"I am sorry fellas, no can do. Unfortunately, it is my civic duty to turn you in to the authorities." Nick turned around and began walking back towards the clubhouse, where he would be able to get the best signal to contact the authorities. Out here on the golf course, by this farthest pond, he possibly would be able to get a signal using his mobile device, but he did not want to waste it on these guys. He needed to save his own signal for finding those last two hidden treasures and the bonus points on this level.

The three men charged toward Nick and barreled him into the pond. Nick landed with a huge splash right on his bottom. His first thought was that he was so thankful his device and his virtual reality glasses were completely waterproof. He stood up so he could chase after the three men, but he saw they were already clear across the golf course. He glanced around and thought he saw something out of the corner of his eye. He settled his virtual reality glasses into place. He smiled to himself. Now he was in the perfect position. He began walking towards the middle of the pond, and he knew he would be able to capture his next hidden treasure.

Over the Fence... or Not

Michael looked around to try to find something he could use to help him climb over the fence. Unfortunately, the houses in this neighborhood had no junk piled anywhere.

"Do you have anything back there that you can use to climb over the fence? Something you can stand on? Or a ladder or a chair you can toss over to me so I could climb over the fence and help you?"

"The only things back here are a lot of branches," a woman shouted.

"Can you stack them up and climb on them? At least then you could get out of there."

He could hear some rustling around on the other side of the fence.

"Come on, Sweetie, if we can stand on these branches, maybe we can get over the fence," a woman said.

The child behind the fence stopped crying, and Michael could hear them gathering items and putting them against the fence near where he was standing.

Michael heard some commotion behind him, and he turned to see what was going on. Two teenage boys were riding up the driveway next door on their bicycles. They dropped their bikes in the driveway and left him lying there while they went into the house.

Michael ran and grabbed a bike, and brought it over and propped against the fence. He climbed on the seat and stood up on it, holding onto the fence, so he was now able to see over the fence. He saw the back yard was full of tree branches, with one huge branch that had fallen but not quite split off from the tree. A woman was on her knees, near a man, Michael couldn't tell if he was alive or dead or awake or asleep, leaning against her. Terry's wife and his daughter were carrying branches over towards the fence where he was.

"I saw you steal that bike!" a man called from the window of the house next-door.

"I'm only borrowing it," Michael said. "It's not going anywhere, just right here."

He hoisted himself over the fence, and landed right in the big pile of branches.

Rescued at Last?

I was so relieved to see Terry's co-worker, Michael, come over the fence into the yard with us.

"Michael!" I said, running over to help him stand up. "I thought that sounded like your voice."

"Daddy!" a little girl's voice called from the other side of the fence. "Are you okay?"

"I'm okay, Sweetheart," Michael called to his daughter. "You wait right there, don't go anywhere, while I help them get over the fence."

"Michael, you have to help us get out of here," I said, pushing Zoey over near the fence.

"That's why I'm here. I could hear shouting from your house, and it sounded like somebody was in trouble."

"We came over here to help our neighbor, Karen, with her husband, but then Karen's daughter wouldn't let us go back through the house, and we have been trapped back here."

"Hey, Mister, can you help me with my husband?" Karen shouted.

"Oh, by the way, Karen, this is Michael. Michael, this is Karen," I said, remembering my manners.

"Now that we have finished with the proper introductions, can you please help me with my husband? I need to get him in the house."

"What's the matter with him?" Michael asked.

Karen said, "This branch fell on him, but he's okay now."

"He doesn't look okay." Michael started to walk over to them.

"I have already called the authorities," the man yelled out the window next door. "They are on their way! They will be here before you can count your fingers!"

"Michael, please, we need to get out of this yard now," I pleaded.

The back door of the house flew open. "Will you stop making so much noise out there? You are disturbing my peace!" the disrespectful teenaged girl yelled at us.

"Daddy, what is going on over there? Are we going to be arrested? I don't want to be arrested!"

"No, Sweetheart, everything is going to be fine. You wait right there by the fence, and we will be there in just a minute."

"Are you going to help me with my husband, or not?" Karen asked. By this time, she was covered in sweat, and her hair was glued to her head.

"Michael, we need to get out of here. Please, help us climb over the fence."

I was already holding Zoey, waiting to boost her over the fence, while Michael was looking around the back yard, from me to Karen, as if trying to decide what to do first. He glanced at the man in the window next door. I guessed that was enough to help him to make his decision. He ran over to where we were standing.

"Here, I will help you go over the fence first. Then I will pass your daughter over the fence to you, then I will try to figure out what to do back here," he said, pointing toward Karen and her husband.

It sounded like a good plan to me, as long as we could get out of this back yard. It seemed like we had been here for hours. I wasn't sure how much time had actually passed.

I set Zoey on the ground. She looked as if she were going to start crying again.

"It's okay, Zoey, Michael is going to help me get over the fence, and then he's going to hand you to me over the fence. Everything is going to be okay. And then we will be able to go back home."

"I want to go home!" Zoey cried.

"Yes, Sweetheart, we are going home, but first we have to climb over the fence."

"I can't climb over the fence!" Zoey cried.

"You don't have to climb over the fence," Michael said, as he was boosting me up. I was able to swing my legs over the fence, and balance there with my legs hanging down, but a bicycle was right beneath me, and I didn't want to fall on it. My foot couldn't reach the seat.

Michael's daughter was waiting there watching me, with a look of fear in her eyes.

"Are we going to be arrested?" she asked.

"No," I managed to say, with the fence pressing into my stomach, "but can you please move this bike out of the way?"

"I'm not supposed to touch anybody else's stuff," she said, "and that is not my bike."

"Mickey!" Michael called from the other side of the fence. "You have my special permission this one time to touch somebody else's bike and move it out of the way."

"Am I going to be arrested?" she asked again.

"No, nobody is going be arrested," her father assured her. "Move the bike out of the way so we can climb over the fence."

"You are all going to be arrested!" the man in the window yelled at us. "You are going to be arrested for disturbing the peace, and for stealing my son's bicycle!"

"We didn't steal it!" Michael's daughter shouted at him. "It's right here!"

She still acted afraid to touch it. It was right in my way so I couldn't drop down from the fence.

"I don't want to get arrested!" she cried.

"You are all going to be arrested!" the man in the window shouted.

"Nobody is going to be arrested!" Michael shouted.

"Will somebody please help me move my husband?" Karen shouted.

"Will everybody be quiet?" Karen's daughter shouted.

"The authorities are on their way right now!" the man shouted.

"Please, move this bicycle out of my way," I begged Michael's daughter. I couldn't quite reach it with my foot to move it myself.

"If I don't touch it, will I still be arrested?" Michael's daughter asked.

"Sweetheart, we need you to move it out of the way," Michael told her.

"Mommy, I can't climb over the fence by myself," Zoey moaned.

"I am going to help you," Michael said, "and I will hand you to your mother as soon as she gets down."

The scream of sirens filled the air.

"Just move the bike a little way, out of my way, so I can get down from here," I told Michael's daughter, using what little breath I had while my stomach was still pressed into the fence.

"I hear the police coming!" she cried.

"So, you need to move the bike out of my way, right now!"

Michael's daughter was frozen with fear, so I let myself down a little bit lower, and I swung my leg with all my might in order to move the bike out of the way. I missed. The motion made me lose my grip on the fence and I fell right onto the bike, landing awkwardly on the ground, and twisting my right ankle in the process. The sound of the sirens grew closer.

"Hand Zoey to me," I yelled, hoping Michael could still hear me. I pushed the bike completely out of my way, and I got close to the fence, standing on my left foot. My right ankle was throbbing painfully.

"Here she comes," Michael called, and Zoey appeared at the

top of the fence. I reached my arms as high I could, and Michael handed her to me. The man in the window was shouting something at us, but I couldn't understand what he was saying because the sirens were so loud. I pulled my daughter close to me, and fell back onto the ground, fortunately shielding her so she didn't get hurt.

At that moment Michael appeared on the ground beside me and in one swift motion he lifted me to my feet, swooped up both Zoey and his daughter into his arms, and we moved as one glob of people across the yard towards our house.

The emergency vehicles came around the corner and stopped right in front of us, blocking our way. A company of young men in uniform who looked to be mere teenagers jumped out of the vehicles and moved toward us. I was happy to see they did not have their weapons drawn.

My ears were ringing even though the sirens were now silent. One of the men was saying something to us, but I couldn't understand him through the ringing in my ears. We all stood still, and recalling what had happened to my husband, I wanted to be sure we didn't say or do the wrong thing. It seemed like they were ready to arrest people for anything these days, not just breaking a law.

The man in the window of the house next door began to shout unintelligibly. Michael set the girls on the ground, and he smiled at the officers. The ringing in my ears was beginning to subside, and I was happy to hear that Michael was composed and sensible when he began to speak to them.

"Good afternoon, officers, I am so glad to see you," he said, extending his hand to them. They looked at it suspiciously but none of them shook it, and he pulled it back to himself. "Our neighbor, Karen, is having a bit of difficulty with her husband in the back yard. We are unable to assist her, because the gate is locked and we can't get over the fence."

A short, fat, young man with black close-shaved hair took out a recorder, and held the microphone in the midst of us so he could capture everything that was being said.

"Why don't you go through the house?" one of the officers asked. He looked like he was about thirteen years old, with blond shaggy hair.

"Because the front door is locked," Michael said, not bothering to explain anything about Karen's daughter.

"You have to arrest those people, all of them! Right now!" the man shouted out the window.

The tallest of the officers, who must have been nearly seven feet tall and probably only weighed 140 pounds, looked at Michael and said, "Why does he think we should arrest you?"

"I have no idea, officer," Michael said politely. "We are only here trying to help."

"He stole my son's bicycle!" the man shouted.

"Is this true?" the tall, skinny officer asked. "Did you steal this man's son's bicycle?"

"No," Michael began, and his daughter interrupted.

"The bike is right over there by the fence," she said, pointing to the bike.

"That is indeed a bicycle, Sir," one of the officers confirmed.

"They have been disturbing my peace all afternoon!" the man in the window shouted. I was thinking that he was disturbing things more than anybody this afternoon, but I didn't say anything.

"We have not been disturbing anyone," Michael said. "We only came to help, but we are unable to do anything to help our neighbor, Karen, because we can't get into her back yard."

Zoey and Michael's daughter looked at him, I hoped they wouldn't say anything.

"You seem to be telling us this in a calm and respectful manner," the tall, skinny guy said.

"Oh, yes, Officer, I am telling you this in a calm and respectful manner," Michael said, in a very calm and respectful manner.

"So, you said you came over here to help the neighbor?" the shaggy blond officer asked.

"Yes, we did," Michael answered.

My ankle was hurting very badly, and I really needed to sit down, so I gritted my teeth and stood there with a grimace on my face that I was hoping could pass for smile.

"That is so not Vinnie Pinchey!" the tall, skinny officer said, looking to the others for confirmation. They began bobbing their heads in agreement.

"Mommy!" Zoey squeaked.

"Shh, not now, Zoey, I said.

The tall, skinny officer glared at Zoey and continued, "Coming out of your own house, entering the property of another, with the intention of helping, is pretty much against the principals and beliefs and attitudes of Vinnie Pinchey. Therefore, I have no choice, but to place all of you under arrest."

"But Officer," I protested, "we didn't actually help her, and she does still need help. Can't you help her? She is right back there, behind the fence." I was hoping to distract them, to get them off track, so they would forget about this ridiculous charge.

"Miss, or should I say, Mrs. Huffy-Puffy," the tall, skinny officer said, "I am saying this in a calm manner and with much respect. Whether or not you committed the act in question or whether you did not commit the act in question or not, is beside the point. You intended to commit the act in question, and therefore you are showing you have no respect for the rules and the principles and beliefs and attitudes of our society. I am going to have to place all of you under arrest, all four of you, in order to make an example of you, as well as to keep this very neighborhood and the streets of our fair city free from such an attitude of rebellion."

"Daddy, is he telling us we are not supposed to help people anymore?" Michael's daughter asked.

"Aha!" said the tall, skinny officer, pointing at her frantically.

"There is proof, right there! Don't you see? You are still

teaching your children contrary to the rules and the principles and beliefs and attitudes of our society. That she would even ask the question is not at all Vinnie Pinchey. We are going to have to take you all downtown. You two are not fit to be parents." He looked at each one of us for a moment.

"Also, it is obvious by looking at you that you are rebels, and you are resisting the order of the land. We knew immediately when we saw you that you are the ones who need to be locked up. I mean, look at you. You let your little girls wear purple and pink, and neither of you is wearing the acceptable color of clothing. You stand out like sore thumbs, throbbing and begging to be iced and wrapped up until you begin to resemble the rest of the normal people in society."

"I knew it!" the man in the window shouted. "I knew something was strange about the clothes they are wearing! We cannot allow people who dress like you people to be running around in our society, rebelling against us in this most blatant display of mutiny!"

Michael and I exchanged glances, and it occurred to me that almost everyone I had seen lately had been wearing dingy green colored clothing. I hadn't really thought about it, but in the back of my mind, I had accepted that most of them had been in the military, or were showing their support for loved ones who were currently serving our country. I wanted to say something, but I held my tongue to keep from getting us in any more trouble.

"I don't think it is necessary to cuff them," the tall, skinny officer told the others. He looked right in Michael's face. "Am I correct in this matter? Will you and your family behave properly, even though you might not have the right attitude, so we don't have to put you in handcuffs?"

"We are not..." Michael began, and I realized they thought we were all in one family and Michael was about to tell them the truth. He changed the rest of his sentence. "We are not a risk, Sir," he said with great dignity. "We will behave. You don't have to put us in handcuffs."

"But Daddy," Michael's daughter cried, "I don't want to be

arrested."

"It's okay, Sweetheart, everything is going to be all right."

The troop of officers began to surround us when suddenly the atmosphere was filled with the sound of screaming and barking. The man with the towel around his waist had been joined by two other men with towels around their waists, and they were running down the street at top speed. This time the dogs were a lot closer, and it looked like one was about to catch and nip the towel of the slowest man.

"What is going on here?" the tall, skinny officer asked, as everyone turned to watch the hilarious sight.

"That is what I would like to know," Michael said.

I was hoping the officers would be distracted and start chasing after the men and the dogs, and leave us alone so we could get across the street and into our house. That did not happen. They stood there and watched the men run down the street as the dogs closed in on them. After the men and the dogs ran around the corner and were out of sight, the officers turned their attention back to our little group. Our girls looked like they were terrified.

"Everything is going to be okay," I said to them quietly.

"Come on, let's go," the tall, skinny officer said to us.

The officers huddled around us, as if we were going to try to escape or something, and they took us over to where the emergency vehicles were parked. I had to limp, because my ankle was so sore.

"What's the matter with you?" one of the other officers asked me. "Are you trying to distract us, so when we are start paying attention to you, the others can escape?"

"No, I recently twisted my ankle and it is very sore right now," I said, wincing at the pain that was shooting up my leg with every step.

"Well, that sounds like a very likely excuse." He held out his hand to stop me and bent down to examine my ankle, which was throbbing and shooting pains up my leg.

94

"Whoa, lady, you have one fat ankle. I would not touch that with a fourteen-foot pole." He shuddered at the idea.

He sure knew how to flatter a woman, I thought, but I didn't say anything out loud. I just smiled at him.

"Does your leg hurt, Mommy?" Zoey asked, concern filling her eyes.

"It will be okay, Sweetie," I assured her.

"You can ride in this one, in the back," the short fat guy with the black hair said, as they directed us to the back door of a van.

We climbed into the van, and I was so relieved to finally sit down on the bench seat. Zoey sat close beside me and Michael and his daughter sat across from us, facing us. I lifted up my sore ankle and began rubbing it gently. That guy had been right – I really did have a fat ankle.

"Daddy," Michael's daughter said, looking around. "Where are the seatbelts?"

"I guess they don't have any in here," Michael said.

"Are they going to arrest us because we are not wearing seatbelts?" she asked.

"I don't have any idea what they are going to do at this point," Michael said. "They haven't officially arrested us for anything yet."

"Why don't they like our clothes, Mommy?" Zoey asked.

"I guess they don't like purple and pink," I said.

"Their eyes must be all messed up, because purple and pink are the prettiest colors of all," she said.

Somebody slammed the door, and we were left alone in the van. It had a type of wire fence between the front seats and the back portion of the van. None of the officers got into the van, either to drive nor to keep an eye on us, and I was trying to think of any way we could get out of here.

"Do you think the back door is locked?" I whispered to

Michael.

He nodded, but didn't make a move to check it.

"My name is Mickey," Michael's daughter said to Zoey. "What is your name?"

Zoey looked at her, afraid to speak.

"It's okay, honey, you can tell her."

"Is she a stranger, Mommy?" Zoey asked me quietly.

"No, she's not a stranger, she is Michael's daughter, and her name is Mickey. Michael works with Daddy. You remember Michael, don't you? Go ahead, tell her what your name is."

"My name is Zoey," she announced.

"Zoey, it is very nice to meet you," Mickey said with a big smile. She stood up and reached out to shake Zoey's hand.

Zoey smiled at her and then turned to me. "Mommy, can Mickey be my new friend?"

"Yes, Dear, she can be your new friend."

"Of course, I will be your friend, Zoey!" Mickey announced joyfully.

Zoey beamed at me, and I knew how important it was to her to have a friend. She hadn't been around any children for the last couple of weeks, ever since she had been asked to permanently leave the school.

"Zoey is getting big," Michael said to me. "The last time I saw her she was only about four years old. How old are you now, Zoey?"

"I am six years old," she said proudly, holding up six fingers to show him.

"I am so glad you showed up right when you did," I said to Michael. "I don't know what we would have done, or how we would have gotten out of the back yard. It was a crazy situation."

"Mommy, I thought we didn't use that word, because it is not nice to say someone is crazy."

"Zoey, we don't use that word to describe people, but in this case, our situation really was crazy."

"How long were you back there?" Michael asked.

"I don't know, but it was entirely too long. Most of the afternoon, anyway. So, what were you doing there, anyway?"

"I came to see about Terry. Is he alright? Where has he been?"

"Haven't you heard? He was arrested almost two weeks ago, and I haven't heard from him since. Oh, I should have thought to call you and tell you."

"He was arrested? What are you talking about? What for? No, I haven't heard anything about it. He stopped coming to work, and I didn't know if he was sick or what. I mean, he had never been sick before, so I didn't know if he was in the hospital, or where he was."

"Well, I want to say that when he was arrested, it was the strangest thing I have ever witnessed, but that was before today happened."

"Terry is always such a stickler for the rules and laws, and he is always obeying every traffic rule and always following directions to the letter for everything. I can't believe he was arrested. What did they arrest him for?"

"That's just it! I don't even know! Someone from Zoey's school called me and said I had to come to school and get her, and this person was acting weird on the phone, talking weird and using odd phrases. So, I drove over to the school, and when I got there, Zoey and Terry were both outside, and the police were there, arresting Terry. They put him in a squad car and took him away. When I called the police station, the person who answered sounded like a twin to the person who called me from the school, and used those weird phrases, too, and I couldn't get any information about Terry, where he was, or why he had been arrested, or anything."

"I have no idea what has gotten into people these days,"

Michael said. "I am not usually around very many people, but it seems like everyone, present company excluded, of course, has gone crazy with a selfish attitude. When I went to the store the other day, every person I came in contact with was extremely rude to me. Even the people working at the store, people I have seen there for years, were so rude to me, and to everyone. Everybody is acting so selfish, like they just want to do their own thing, and they don't even care about other people, about helping other people, or even listening to other people."

"I haven't gone anywhere lately," I said. "I have been staying home, and trying to keep a normal life at home for Zoey and me. I have also been hoping I would get a phone call from Terry or from somebody who can give me some information about him."

"I had no idea he had been arrested," Michael said, shaking his head. "I can't believe it. I mean, I believe what you are telling me, but it's an impossible situation to believe. Terry is the last person in the entire world I would ever think would be arrested."

"What about me, Daddy?" Mickey asked. "Did you think I would be arrested?"

"I never thought I would be arrested," Zoey said.

"No," Michael said with a chuckle, "I did not think you two would ever be arrested, either."

"I wonder what is going on?" I asked. "Do you think those officers went to help Karen and her husband? I don't hear anything happening outside."

"I wish we could get out of here," Michael said. "They didn't take down our names or anything. Maybe if we can open the back door, we can make a run for it."

"I don't think I can run on my ankle," I said. "It is really aching right now."

"Oh, that's right, I forgot. Maybe if we can get the door open, I can help you. All we have to do is get to your house. If they're not looking, I'm sure we can make it. You girls are pretty good runners, aren't you?"

"I am a really fast runner," Zoey said.

"Daddy, you know I can run fast," Mickey said.

Michael stood up and went to the back door of the van. He tried the latch, and it was unlocked. He slowly opened the door and stuck his head out to look around.

"The officers are nowhere in sight," he told us. "I am sure we can make it before they see us. Girls, I want you to run as fast as you can across the street to Zoey's house and wait for us on the porch by the front door."

"Daddy, do you want us to hide from the police? We can hide on the porch where they can't see us," Mickey said.

"Yes, good idea," Michael said. "Come on, let's go." He motioned for them to move.

The girls leaped up and were at the door instantly, while I struggled to get to my feet. I was unable to put any weight on my foot, since my ankle was killing me. I hopped on my left foot the few steps to the door.

"Okay, let's go," Michael said, opening the door enough for us to get through. The girls jumped out, landed on the street, and quickly ran across to our house.

Michael got out of the van and helped me as I sat on the edge and eased myself down to the ground. I put my arm around his shoulders while he put his arm around my waist, and I hopped on one foot all the way across the street, keeping my balance by leaning on him. I looked to see the girls already on the porch, peeking at us while they were hiding.

We made it to the steps and Michael helped me up, one, two, three. I fished my key out of my pants pocket and Michael opened the screen door. My heart was pounding so hard, I dropped my keys while I was trying to stick the house key in the lock, and they landed with a crash on the porch. Michael leapt over and picked up the keys before I could even bend down to get them, and he handed a them to me. I got the key into the lock, and was just turning it when I heard a shout from across the street.

"Hey! The prisoners are getting away!"

My hand was shaking so hard, I was unable to get the door unlocked and open before we were again surrounded by these young men in ugly green informs. I almost felt like crying, but I knew I could not break down in front of Zoey.

"Come on, come on," the tall, skinny guy told us. "So, you thought you could get away?"

"No," I lied, my mind racing much more quickly than I was able to at the time, "my daughter had to go to the bathroom, and you didn't have any facilities in the back of the van."

I looked at Zoey with an expression that told her not to say a word, don't tell them that I am not telling the truth.

"Oh, well, in that case," the tall, skinny guy said, "we better her let her go to the bathroom, because we have a very long drive ahead of us. Open the door, and we will all go in. Does anyone else need to use the bathroom while we are here?"

I fumbled with the keys and opened the door, trying to think of a way to get out of this mess. I let the girls go in the house first. I hobbled in behind them, and Michael and the other men followed us inside. We assembled in the living room.

"Zoey, you and Mickey go to the bathroom first. Is that okay, Officer?" I asked.

"Yes, of course, we always have to let the little girls go first," the tall, skinny guy said. You, lady, you go after them, but don't you think about trying any funny stuff, like climbing out the window or anything. Hanks, you go around to the back of the house and make sure nobody climbs out of the windows."

"Yes, Sir," Hanks said. He was as stubby as a fireplug, the buttons on his uniform about to burst open. He turned to me. "What is the best way to get to your back yard? We had an impossible situation trying to get into your neighbor's back yard across the street. We never did get into the yard. I'm not sure if anyone even needed help over there. Maybe you were making it all up? Well, it doesn't matter, we have you now, in any case."

"Just go that way, through the kitchen, and you will see the door to the back yard," I told him.

As I turned to head toward the bathroom, one of the officers said, "Hey, this place is pretty nice. I'm going to sit down and relax for a few minutes. Hey, where is your remote? And where is your large screen? Don't you have one in here?"

"No, we don't have a large screen in here," Michael said, confirming that a large screen was not somehow hidden in this room.

I glanced back and saw the officer plop down on the couch. He took another look around the room and then he pulled his mobile device out of his pocket. "Does anybody want to join me in a VP challenge?"

"I will," the tall, skinny guy said, pulling out his mobile device.

I looked over at Michael and shrugged, wondering what kind of challenge they were talking about, hoping they might be distracted, to get their attention off of us.

"Yeah, go ahead, make yourself at home," Michael said, nodding at me. "Go on and use the bathroom."

I figured this was his way of telling me he had things covered here, so I went to check on the girls, hopping all the way.

I was trying to think of any way we could escape from this situation. None of the officers were guarding us. If we went out the back door, we would be trapped in the back yard, much like we had been at Karen's house across the street; and besides, Hanks was out there. If we went through the door into the garage, we could get in the car, I could open the garage door, and we could drive away before they knew we were gone. But where could we go? Michael was in the front room with the officers. But still, I had a feeling that if I could get away with the girls, maybe we could go over to Michael's house and hide there – if Mickey had a key, and if I was able to drive with my ankle in such pain. Maybe I could drive to the hospital and have someone take a look at my ankle. Now, that was beginning to sound like the best option, and then we could figure out what to do from there. I knew Michael was hoping I would get the girls out of here, with or without him.

As I was standing outside the bathroom door, waiting for Zoey and Mickey to finish, I stuck my hand in my pocket to be sure I still had my car keys. I was sure I would have enough time to get all of us into the car and get out of there before these young men even missed us.

"Zoey, are you finished in the bathroom?" I called through the door.

"I don't have to go!" she said. "I am waiting for Mickey to wash her hands."

"You need to go anyway," I told her. "Just go, because it might be a long time before we get a chance to go again."

"Okay, Mommy," she agreed. "I will try."

"Good girl," I said, formulating the plan in my mind. My purse was on top of the refrigerator in the kitchen, and I had plenty of money in it. I would get the girls, grab my purse, take them quietly out the garage door, and maybe I could even get Michael to go out with us; if only I could get him away from the officers.

"Michael, can you come here for a minute?" I asked, taking a chance he would be allowed to come alone.

He appeared beside me in an instant. "What is it?" he asked, a look of worry on his face.

"I have a plan," I whispered.

"Yes, we have more toilet paper in the garage," he said loudly.

I was sure he had guessed my plan, and we would be able to make an escape from these people who were holding us hostage in my own house, when one of the officers appeared behind Michael.

"Do you have anything to drink?" he asked, as if we were hosting a social event.

"Yes, sure, look in the refrigerator, right through there, in the kitchen," I said. "We have milk, water, juice, and I think there might still be some soda in there."

"What about the hard stuff?" he asked.

Another officer sauntered around the corner. "Did I hear you say you have soda? I am so thirsty. I could use a soda. What kind do you have?"

"I don't know," I said, looking into Michael's eyes, trying to communicate to him telepathically, which, by the way, was not at all working. "Look for yourself. I don't drink it, but I think we have some in there."

He opened the refrigerator door and looked inside. "Do you have any popcorn?" he asked.

"Popcorn?" Michael asked, shrugging. "You want popcorn?"

"Yeah, it sounds really good right now," the officer said.

"Oh, yes, I could use some popcorn," another officer said, coming to the kitchen. "Do you have any? That does sound good."

"I am not sure if we have any popcorn in the house," Michael replied.

"What about the hard stuff?" the other officer asked, rejecting my offer of milk, water, juice or soda.

"Hard stuff popcorn?" one of the officers laughed. "You are crazy, dude."

"No, we don't have any hard liquor," I answered. "We don't drink the hard stuff."

"Are you serious?" he gasped. "What is the matter with you people? I can't believe it! You really DO have a problem! I should write you up for that, too."

The bathroom door opened and Zoey and Mickey came out. I felt as if we were missing our opportunity to get away from this insane situation. I looked again at Michael, but he nodded for me to go into the bathroom.

"Maybe you can put a wrap or something on your ankle," he suggested, as I was closing the door.

That was actually a great idea, but I knew we didn't have any type of bandage to use to wrap a wound. None of us had ever had this type of injury before, and Terry wasn't the type to buy a bunch of medical supplies we did not need. I turned on the water to make some noise while I tried to think. Terry was the type to buy a first aid kit, though, and we had one in the car! So, we now had a reason to go out to the car, to get a bandage for my ankle. Michael would have to be the one to do the wrapping, we could get into the car with the girls and then we would be able to drive away from these young officers and their insanity!

To Be Forgotten

"Hey! Is anybody out there?" Terry called through the little slot in his door. "Hello? Hello?"

Although Terry could not be sure how long he had been in solitary confinement, and he didn't know if it were day or night, or how many days had passed since he had seen anyone, he knew it must've been quite a while, because he was really getting hungry. His stomach was growling and he had a terrible headache. He was able to drink water from the small sink in his room, but he was sure it had been at least several days since he had had any food.

"Did you forget about me? I am still in here! Hello? Is anybody out there? Am I the only one here?"

He was answered with complete silence. He had no idea what was happening, or why he had been abandoned in this little cell, but he knew it was against his constitutional rights. Even prisoners had to be fed, even murderers. Even the worst kind of criminals had the right to eat, even when they were on death row.

He felt around until found the sink, turned on the faucet, and he drank as much water as he possibly could.

He sat back down on the hard, little cot and he again began to pray out loud.

"Dear God, I don't understand Your ways, or why You have me here right now, but I am asking You to take care of my wife and our daughter until the time when You bring me home to them. I thank You because everything You do is right, and You know the end from the beginning. I am in Your hands. Comfort and strengthen me. I love You. Help me, please, help me. I thank You for it in advance. In the precious name of Jesus, I pray. Amen."

Boys Will Still Be Boys

Four teenage boys sat around Denny's room, each engaged with his mobile device, and each wearing his dull green jacket over his dull green shirt.

"I am going to get it!" Chuck shouted. "I am going to the next level! I am ahead of you all, you losers!"

"This game is absolutely major," Denny said, maneuvering his mobile device, in order to score the most points. "This is, oh, wow, look at my display of rewards! You chumps, oh, wow, now I see why it's better not to be talking while in the middle of – oh! oh! Wow, this is major!"

"Are you guys getting hungry?" Lenny asked, setting his device aside, as his stomach made a loud grumbling noise. "I could really use something that is not a flavored shake, and not a pile of overcooked vegetables, the only things my mom will make any more. Don't tell anyone this, but I would be completely satisfied if I never ate another rutabaga in my life."

"Yes, I am hungry! Anything else sounds good to me," Morris agreed, just as he completed round one of his challenge. His eyes were bothering him, after staring at the small screen for so many hours. "I could really eat some real food."

"Oh! There it goes!" Chuck shouted triumphantly. "I did it! I did it! I am so far in the lead, as usual! You guys will never be able to catch me now!" He locked in his score and looked around the dark room. The image of his screen was burned into his brain, and all he could see was the brightness of the screen, everywhere he looked. He blinked several times, but even with his eyes closed, he could see the little rectangle-shaped image.

"Does your mom have any other kind of food in the house?" Morris asked. Although they could only be cool if they were Vinnie

Pinchey, they had agreed among themselves that they would not say those words. None of the boys on the Vinnie Pinchey program ever said the words, although the influence was absolutely everywhere. "How about some chips, or some hot dogs, or burritos, or something like that?"

"No, we have already wiped out all of those kinds of things," Denny said. "The only edible things we have in the kitchen are the shakes and all those weird vegetables everyone is eating these days."

"I honestly feel like eating something else," Lenny said, "before I starve to death."

"I know, me too," agreed Morris. "Our kitchen is about like yours. My mom won't buy anything anymore that is not on the program."

"It is so weird, you know?" Lenny said. "We are all on the same program, I mean, everyone is on the same program, but it is not working out so well for us. We should be able to do whatever we want to do, but when we want to eat, we can't find the good stuff we want to eat."

"I know what you are saying," Chuck said. "We don't have to go to school if we don't want, and we don't want, so here we are, hanging out, like we do every day, and that is so cool, but what happens when we want to eat something that is not available to us? Something really good and snacking, you know? We are still growing boys, I mean, we are practically young men, and they can't treat us like we don't need a nice variety of food! I'm saying, Man, I really need to eat something substantial, like French fries and nachos and onion rings!"

"When was the last time any of you had a good burger, I mean, a nice, big, juicy, tasty burger, packed with tomatoes and pickles and onions and lettuce and cheese?" Morris asked.

"Oh, Morris, dude, you are making me faint, Man, my lips are watering, just thinking about it," Lenny said, leaning back in his chair.

"That sounds so good!" Denny said. "Where can we get anything like that? All those kinds of restaurants have either closed or gone on the program. If I have to eat another veggie burger with a lettuce bun, I am going to fade away, I am warning you. If you see me lying on the ground, all faded away, you will know why."

"I heard a rumor," Chuck said slyly, lowering his voice, "there are still a couple of those old-fashioned drive-thrus on the other side of town."

"Really? Are you serious?" Morris asked. "Don't you be joking about something as critical as this, Man. I mean, this is the most important thing you have ever said, I mean, lately, so you better not be kidding around."

"No, seriously!" Chuck insisted. "It is a little known fact, but nobody from this side ever goes over there any more, you know, because they don't want to go there."

"Well, that is a fact," Lenny said, nodding his head. "Who would ever want to go over to the other side of town, anyway?"

The four boys looked at each other, from one to another, the idea churning in their minds. Lenny's stomach growled loudly.

"I do!" the four shouted simultaneously.

THE GREAT GARAGE ESCAPE

By the time I came out of the bathroom, the young officers had settled into our house like long lost relatives. Three were sitting at the kitchen table, eating and drinking, three were out in the back yard goofing around and playing, and four more were in the living room doing something with their mobile devices. None of them were paying any attention to us at all. Michael, Mickey and Zoey were waiting for me in the hallway, outside the bathroom door.

"Michael, can you wrap my ankle?" I asked, loud enough for everyone to hear. "I think the first aid kit is out in the car, in the garage."

"Do you want me to go out and get it?" Michael asked.

"No, let's both go out and you can wrap it there," I suggested. I motioned for the girls to follow us into the garage.

Zoey looked at me anxiously, and I smiled to try to relieve her fears. The four of us went into the garage, and I realized I didn't have my purse with me. It was still on top of the refrigerator. But I did have my car keys in my pocket, so I pulled them out now.

"Get in the car," I whispered loudly. The others didn't hesitate. I motioned for Michael to get on the driver's side, while I lowered myself into the passenger seat. I handed him the keys.

"Let's go," I told him. "They are all preoccupied, they are not paying any attention to us or what we are doing." I pressed the button to open the garage door.

"I noticed none of them had a gun," Michael said, starting the car. As the garage door came open, I looked back and saw Michael's car was in the driveway, right behind our car.

"Oh no! Your car is right there, in the way! We are not going to be able to get out!"

"It's okay, I can get around it," Michael said. "Fasten your seat belts, girls."

Michael was able to maneuver around his own car by driving on our front lawn, and we were finally free from the house, away from those young officers.

"Yay!" the girls shouted together.

"Daddy, you did it! Where are we going?" Mickey asked.

"I don't know yet, I just want to get away from here, as fast as we can," Michael said, as he drove out of our neighborhood.

"I'm sorry we had to leave them in your house. I didn't know what else to do. We had to get away from those guys. I don't think they are real police officers. I have no idea who they are. I think they are guys who are playing, like they are just doing this because they want to do it. There is a lot of that kind of attitude going around lately."

"That's fine, you are right. We had to get away from them, no matter what." I put my head back on the headrest, feeling like I could finally breathe. This had been one horrible day, and I just wanted things to get back to normal.

"Oh, yes," Michael said. "This whole thing seems like trouble."

The Only Way to Get from Here to There

"How are we going to get there?" Chuck asked.

"Do you even know where this place is?" Lenny asked.

"Well, I sort of know the general area where it is," Chuck said. "It is on the other side of town, kind of near one of the parks, over by Peach Tree Lane, from what I heard."

"What good does that do us? It's too far to walk clear across town. By the time we get there, I would probably starve to death anyway," Lenny said.

"We can drive," Morris said. "Denny, your mom has a car, doesn't she? And she is not using it now, right?"

"Yeah, she has one," Denny said. "But I haven't ever driven it."

"It's okay," Morris said. "I can drive."

"You are going to drive my mom's car?" he asked. "When did you learn how to drive?"

"I have always known how to drive," Morris explained. "Some people have to learn, but some people, like me, already know. It's in my bones."

"Well, I hope it is also in your brain, and in your hands and feet," Lenny said, laughing loudly.

"This is something we all want to do, isn't it?" Chuck asked.

"Well, yeah," they agreed.

"So, aren't we supposed to be able to do whatever we want to do?" Chuck said.

"That is the way of the day," Morris admitted. "We should not have to deny ourselves anything we want to do. We should be able to do anything we want to do. And since all four of us want this, there is a multiplication factor there that says we have permission to do this."

"You do have a point there," Lenny agreed, nodding his head. "Four of us all want the same thing, so there should be nothing to stop us from getting what we want. It's like you said, we have a multiplication factor of four."

"So, what are we waiting for?" Morris asked. "Where does your mom keep the car keys?"

"There's a spare key in the den," Denny said.

"Let's go!" Chuck said. "I am getting hungrier by the second, and the more we sit around here talking about it, the more hungrier I am." His stomach growled to confirm it. "Man, look at me! I am wasting away! If I don't get some real food in me, I am going to be skin and bones before you know it!"

"You're not the only one," Lenny said, his stomach echoing the growl of his friend's.

"You are sure you know how to drive?" Denny asked Morris, as they thumped down the stairs.

"I know how to drive better than you know how to sleep, my friend," Morris assured him.

What Is Normal Life These Days Again?

"Daddy, I am really hungry," Mickey announced from the back seat.

"Me, too," Zoey said. "Mommy, when are we going to eat?"

"Do you mind if we go get something to eat now?" I asked Michael.

"Yes, sure, I am hungry too," he agreed. "Where do you want to go?"

"I don't know, anywhere sounds good to me. I could eat almost anything right now, after the day we have had today.

"Daddy, can we go to that restaurant we went to one time?" Mickey asked.

"Which one are you talking about?" Michael asked.

"You know, that one I really like that had all of that really good food."

"Which one was it?" Michael asked. "We have been to a lot of different restaurants."

"I don't know the name of it, but the food was really good. You like it too. Don't you remember?"

"I don't know which one you're talking about," Michael said.

"You know, that one I really like!" Mickey insisted.

"It doesn't matter to me, let's find a restaurant that is open and go there," I said.

"I hope we can find an open restaurant around here," Michael said. "So many of them either have weird hours or they have closed completely."

"It has been so long since I've been to a restaurant, I didn't know that," I said.

"Well, let's go to one that would be open right now," Michael said.

"Is it one I like, Daddy?" Mickey asked.

"Yes, Mickey, I am sure you will like this one. I don't know if you have been there before, but I know you will like it. They have good food."

"What is the name of it?" Mickey asked.

"I can't remember the name, but you will like it, Sweetheart. I guarantee you will like it. If you don't like it, we will go someplace else."

"Any place sounds good to me," I said.

"Me too!" Zoey added.

Michael made a left turn into an area of town where I had never been before.

"It is a couple miles ahead," he said. "I know you are all going to like it."

IN SEARCH OF THE PERFECT SNACK

"Man, watch where you are going!" Denny said to Morris, as he was weaving in the car back and forth on the street.

"I am watching everything! Calm down, Buddy," Morris said. "I am just getting a feel for the car and how it handles. Just sit back and enjoy the ride."

"I would enjoy the ride if you would stop driving like a maniac," Denny said, gritting his teeth.

"Man, this is nothing!" Chuck said. "You should see my brother drive. It is like a roller coaster and a dive plane all in one."

"And that is one reason why I would never let your brother drive my mother's car," Denny said.

"Relax, Man, I have everything under control." Morris was able to stop the car from wavering from side to side, but that didn't stop Denny from keeping his eyes peeled.

"I hope you all have on your seatbelts," Denny warned.

"Come on, Dude, it's like he said," Lenny said. "Relax and enjoy the ride."

"That's easy for you to say," Denny commented. "It's not your mother's car."

"Yeah, and that's a good thing," Lenny said laughing. "Her car won't even make it out of our garage right now. My dad took off all the tires and put them on his car."

"What did he do that for?" Chuck asked.

"I don't know, Man," Lenny shrugged. "I guess he wanted to do it, Man. These days, he does whatever he wants to do, pretty much like everybody else."

"Yeah, I know what you mean," Morris said. "My dad has been staying over at his girlfriend's place for the past two weeks. I haven't even seen him. But that is what he wants to do, so I guess he has the right to do it, like I have the right to do what I want to do. Like we all do!"

"You said, it, Morris," Chuck agreed. "We all have the right to do whatever we want to do, and that is the way it is, like it or not! And I am telling you, I like it. Forget about all that other stuff. Why should we have to do what we don't want to do? That doesn't make any sense. Everyone is a lot happier this way, especially in my family. I mean, I haven't heard my mom and my sister fight, not even once, since the beginning of this programming season. My mom knows what my sister wants to do, my sister knows what she wants to do, so why should they argue about it?"

"So, what is your sister doing?" Lenny asked, with a little more curiosity than he should have about his friend's sister.

"Hey! What my sister wants to do is none of your business, Buddy!" Chuck shouted. "You better stay away from her, I am warning you."

"Man, I wouldn't go near your sister if she were the last girl on earth," Lenny said. "That is, unless she and I were the only two people left on earth, then, you know, we would have to get to know each other better."

Chuck and Lenny started a fist fight in the back seat while Denny kept his eyes on the road, peeled for any little infraction Morris might make.

"Cut it out!" Lenny shouted.

"You started it!"

"I did not!"

"You leave my sister alone!"

"I told you, I don't want anything to do with your sister!"

"Hey! Guys!" Denny yelled nervously. "Stop it! Can't you see, I'm driving!"

The boys in the back seat stopped hitting each other and started laughing.

"I got this," Morris said, cool as an ice cube, as he turned the corner. "Chuck, where is this place supposed to be? I thought you said it was on Peach Tree Lane. Man, I am so hungry! I am going to order everything they have on the menu!"

"No, I said it was BY Peach Tree Lane, but not right ON Peach Tree Lane," Chuck said. "That's the street, right back there. Go back! Go back one street, and there it is, right there."

Morris swung the car around to make a U-turn.

At that very moment, all four of their mobile devices began to emit various irritating tones. They all reached into their pockets to see what kind of alert they were getting.

"Man, I hope nobody beat my high score," Chuck said, logging in to his device.

"Then why would we all get notified?" Morris asked, taking his eyes off the road to read his urgent alert. We are not even—"

All four boys, none of whom were wearing a seat belt, were knocked unconscious when Denny's mom's car smashed into the car that was in its own lane, directly in their path.

I Thought I Could

"The restaurant is right around this corner—hold tight! Help, Lord!" Michael shouted, as a car headed directly toward them, not slowing one bit. Michael swerved to the right and slammed on the brakes, but the other car barreled right into the front of our car. My eyes were frozen on that car as I saw what was happening, and I was helpless as this nightmare unraveled right in front of me.

Mickey and Zoey began to cry, which I felt was a good thing – they were both still conscious and able to react to the situation. My seat belt had locked up and I was unable to move my body. I slowly turned my head, feeling a great aching in my neck; but still, I was able to move my head.

Michael was slumped over to one side, his eyes closed. "Michael! Michael!" I screamed. I couldn't move any further because a portion of the car had been crushed right above my legs, pinning them down, making my earlier ankle injury ache like crazy.

The crying of the girls was becoming overwhelming, taking me over, turning into a wailing, a siren, and I felt like closing my eyes to make it all go away. I was so very tired. All I needed was a little nap. Everything would be okay, if I could just shut my eyes for a moment. My energy had been completely drained... I was so tired... Everything could wait for a few minutes while I rested, couldn't it?

THE NIGHTMARE RETURNS

"Bzzzz... Bzzzz... Bzzzz... Ahhhh... Mmmm... Come on, lady, come on, get out!" a strangely familiar voice was shouting. "No use faking it, we have you now!"

I thought I had been dreaming, having a nightmare, but as I opened my eyes, here I still was, trapped in our car, and we had been involved in a car accident. My legs were still pinned, but my seat belt was not holding me in place. As a matter of fact, my seat belt was gone.

I realized the girls had stopped crying, so I slowly turned to check on them. As I moved my head, I noticed Michael was no longer in the driver's seat and his door was wide open. I tried to call his name, but my mouth and tongue decided to not respond to my brain. I turned my head a bit further and saw the back seat was empty.

Zoey! Where was she? Where was my daughter?

"Come on, Lady, I said, get out of the car! You are perfectly fine! Get moving, right now! I mean it, Lady!"

"Ohhh," I was able to muster, the closest thing I could say to Zoey's name.

"GET OUT!"

"Sooo," I said, barely a whisper, needing to go back to sleep, but even more, I needed to know where our daughter was, and that she was all right.

I turned my head in the other direction, to my right, and I was suddenly looking into the face of that tall, skinny officer we had left at our house a few lifetimes ago, or sometime during my previous nightmare. The car door was open, and he was staring at me, as if somehow this accident had been my fault.

"Get out of there, now!" he shouted.

"Stuuu…" I said, trying with all my might to tell him I was stuck. My eyes were speaking volumes, but obviously, he could not understand their language.

"Stop making trouble!" he yelled at me. "You are nothing but a real trouble-maker! We have had nothing but trouble from you all day! How did you get here, anyway? I thought we left you back at the house, but here you are, clear across town, when we got the report of an accident. You have to make trouble everywhere you go, don't you?"

I shook my head slightly, which was about all I could do. I looked down at my legs, and finally, he got the message.

"We got a stuck one here!" the boy called out loudly.

A few of the young officers who had been in our house appeared beside the car.

"Whoa!" one guy said. "She really is stuck there, isn't she?"

"It doesn't look like your legs are bleeding," another guy said, leaning in to examine the situation. "How are we going to get her out of here?"

"Mommy!" Zoey called out, much to my relief. "Mommy, are you okay?"

"Yes," I said, in the faintest voice I had ever used in my life, yet with all my might, it was the loudest I could possibly be.

She pushed her way between the much bigger boys to get to me.

"Zo," I whispered.

She turned to the boys who were standing behind her, and I could imagine the look on her face as she asked them, "Can you get my mommy out for me? I need my mommy."

I was expecting some kind of sarcastic remark, but instead, they were touched by her request. The tall, skinny guy squatted down so he was face-to-face with Zoey. "We are going to get her out for you," he promised, looking directly into her eyes.

"Thank you, Mr. Policeman," she said politely.

I thought I saw the trace of a tear in his eye. He stood up and turned to the others. "She called me 'Mr. Policeman.'"

Her remark stirred them into action. They started moving about, this way and that. One brought a big toolbox over, and someone got into the seat behind me and started working. Another guy used some kind of prying tool to remove the glove box, which was a great relief to have off my thighs. My legs felt somewhat numb, but I didn't think I had any new injuries, thank God.

The young men worked together until finally my legs were free. Several of them helped me get out of the car, holding me up, since my strength was almost gone.

"Come over here," the tall, skinny guy said. To my horror, I saw they were taking us to the same van from which we had escaped earlier. I desperately wanted to get away from there, but I could not move on my own, and Zoey was attached to my arm. I tried to stand still, with no success. They pulled me along, against my will.

"It's okay, Mommy, they are nice," Zoey said.

Could she not remember what had happened with these very same guys earlier in the day? At this point, it didn't matter, because I was too weak to resist.

"Come on, into the van," the tall, skinny guy said, as he opened the back door. "Help them get in, fellas."

One guy lifted Zoey into the van, and it took at least three of them to get me inside and over to the bench, the same bench where we had been sitting earlier. As my eyes adjusted to the darkness, I was relieved to see Michael and Mickey sitting across from us. In my state of mind, I had forgotten about them for a few minutes. I was glad to see they were here, and, I hoped, they were okay.

"Michael," I whispered, still unable to speak with my normal voice.

"Oh, you have no idea how glad I am to see you," he said. That was when I noticed he had some kind of cloth wrapped around his left arm. "Are you okay? They said you were unconscious. I was really praying for you."

"You were..." I began. The rest of the sentence, whatever I had been planning to say, was unimportant, now that we were here together.

"That car just whipped around in front of us," he said. "I am so sorry. I couldn't do anything. It all happened too fast."

"Are they..." was all I was able to say. Fortunately, Michael was able to finish my thought.

"Teenagers," he said. "I guess they were too young to drive, out on a joy ride or something, and they happened to mess up right in our path. I think they are going to be okay. Some guys took them to the hospital to get checked. If they were my sons, I am telling you, they would be grounded for life."

"Daddy, what is grounded?" Mickey asked.

"It is something I truly hope you never have to experience," he said.

"Is it a bad thing?" she asked.

"It happens when you do a bad thing," he told her.

"I never want to do anything bad, Daddy," she said solemnly.

"Me neither!" Zoey agreed.

"Are we under arrest again, Daddy?" Mickey asked.

"Well, they didn't say anything about it to me," he said. "I guess I blacked out for a few minutes, but besides a nasty cut on my arm, I am okay." He leaned closer to our side of the van and lowered his voice. "You know, these guys, these officers, something is pretty strange about them. They don't have guns, they don't have radios, they don't have badges. They don't act like they know what they are doing. All they have done is boss us around, but they have not read us our rights or told us we are under arrest."

"And they ate lots of our food and drank soda at our house," Zoey added.

Michael smiled at her. "Yes, they certainly did."

"What are they doing now, Daddy?" Mickey asked.

"I don't really know," he said, "but I think they are trying to figure out what to do with us."

"Where is the am-blee-ance, Daddy?" Mickey asked.

"The ambulance?" he said, puzzled. "You're right, Mickey! I was so shook up, I didn't even realize until now, but they took the teenagers to the hospital in a van like this one. I have not seen an ambulance here. Don't you think that is odd?"

I was thinking that this entire day had pretty much been odd, but I could not get my mouth, my voice to cooperate, so I just nodded.

"So, can we go and get something to eat now, Mommy?" Zoey asked.

An Odd Ending to an Odd Day

I must have dozed off in the van, so I had no idea how long we had been riding when we finally stopped. I tried to see out through the front window, but it was now dark, and I could not see a thing. As the world came back into focus, I could hear the driver and the other young man talking, even though I couldn't see them from where I was sitting.

"Is this the place?"

"Yeah, from what I heard."

"It looks like it is abandoned."

"Yep. It looks to be deserted all right."

"So, what are we going to do?"

"Take them inside. Leave them here."

I tried to see Michael's face, but it was too dark inside the van to see anything.

"Did you call ahead?"

"No, did you?"

"No, why do you think I asked you?"

"The same reason I asked you."

"And what would be that reason?"

"So, I would know!"

"And that was my reason, as well. So, I would know! And then we would both know, if you and I know, you know."

"Yeah, I know. So, what should we do?"

"Take them inside."

"But what if no one else is here?"

"Doesn't matter. This is where we bring the rebels. That is what I heard. Or, no, I read it somewhere. Doesn't matter! We can't take them back and we can't just drop them off somewhere."

"They have those two little girls."

"Yeah, it would be much better to leave them here. At least they would have shelter, and they would be away from society, as it should be."

"Oh, yeah, we can't have their kind wandering free, disturbing our society and not conforming to the order of the day."

"You are right about that, my friend."

"And we don't actually want anything bad to happen to them."

"On the contrary. We should not even care one bit about them, about what happens to them. I mean, is that what we want to do?"

"Not at all. What I really want to do is to get something to eat."

"Maybe they have something here we can eat."

"Man, it looks like no one has been here in ages."

"Let's go inside and see if we can find something to eat."

"Shouldn't we let them out first?"

"No, I want to go get something to eat first."

"I want to let them out."

"What if they run away?"

"Where are they going to go, all the way out here in the desert, in the dark like this, without a car?"

"You're right. They can't go anywhere."

"Maybe they are hungry."

"Yeah, I thought I heard the little girl saying that."

"No, I want to go find some food first, and then we can let them out."

"Okay, let's go. Sounds like a good idea to me. I'm starving."

They got out of the van, and slammed the doors.

"Did you hear that?" Michael whispered to me.

"Yes," I said, finally able to speak, a bit above a whisper. "Do you know where we are?"

"Only that we are way out in the desert," he answered. "I was not able to see any landmarks on the way here."

"Mommy, I am really hungry now," Zoey cried.

"I am hungry too, Daddy," Mickey said.

"Can we get out, and go see if we can find something to eat?" I asked.

"I can't think of any better plan," Michael said. "Can you walk?"

"I can if you help me," I said. My ankle was still throbbing pretty badly.

"Daddy can help you!" Mickey announced.

Before we could get out of the van, the back door flew open and the two young men were standing there.

"Oh, good, you are ready to go," the taller one said, helping us out of van. I stood with all my weight on my left foot.

"Where are we going?" Zoey asked.

"Right here!" he told her. "You are going right here, and as a matter of fact, you are already right here."

"Do they have food here?" she asked. "I'm hungry."

"Of course, they have food," he said, pointing to a dark building a bit of a distance from us. "Right in there, they have lots of food. You are going to love it."

"I hope so," she said. "I am really hungry."

"It looks pretty dark," I said, holding Zoey back, so she wouldn't try to run over to the building ahead of us.

"Wait a minute," Michael said. "Isn't this the old prison? Did you bring us to a prison? Are you planning to leave us here, at the prison? You never even arrested us! I want my lawyer! I have the right to talk to my lawyer!"

"Why is it so dark, Daddy?" Mickey asked.

"Hey, you guys do whatever you want," the taller officer told us. "We are outta here. Have a good life!"

The two boys darted around us, but Michael grabbed one of them by the hand as he was trying to get by us.

"You tell me right now, what is going on here! Are we under arrest or not? Are you even real policemen?"

The boy was able to get his arm away from Michael, and he called to us as he jumped into the van, "Ha-ha-ha! We are not policemen! We are just doing what we want to do! Ha-ha-ha! We never said you were under arrest! Ha-ha-ha! Wasn't that fun? I always wanted to be a policeman!"

The driver added, laughing, as he put the van in gear and gunned the engine, "We are only fourteen!"

The van whipped around in the dust and was gone.

You Are Not Alone

Terry was lying on the hard, lumpy cot in his cell, not sure if he might be dreaming, or was he actually awake, when he heard the sound of voices.

"Hey! I'm in here! Hello! Is anybody there?" he called out, as loud as his weakened voice would allow. He listened, but did not hear anyone again. "Did you forget about me? I am still here!"

He picked up his metal dish, the one that had had his most recent meal in it – when was it? Days ago, or weeks ago? – and he began banging it on the steel door. After a moment or two of making as much noise as he possibly could, he stopped to listen again.

At this moment, he heard a voice telling him, "I am with you. You are not alone."

"God, is that you? Can you open this door for me?" he asked. Then he began to shout again. "Hello! Hello! Hey! I am still here! Good morning, or good afternoon or good evening! Here I am! Hello!"

He was answered with silence.

"Come on, someone, please! How long are you going to hold me here?" he called out. "Hellllooooo! Can you hear me? Is anyone there? I am still in here!"

He stopped yelling as a pure peace enveloped him. He felt a warmth tingling all over his body. He was sure he was not alone, and he was not going to die alone in here. He knew, he believed with all his heart, this was not his time to die, and he was going to walk out of this place.

He very calmly walked over to the door. He gave it a little push, and, miraculously, the door opened.

THE ONLY PLACE TO GO

"Let's go inside and see if we can get something to eat," I said to Michael.

"Will they arrest us and lock us up?" Mickey asked.

"No, Sweetheart, they won't," Michael assured her, as he put his arm around me, to help me walk the final fifty yards or so to the building. I prepared myself to hop on my left foot the whole way.

"Do you promise, Daddy?" she asked. "I don't want to be arrested."

"I promise, I won't let them arrest any of us," he said.

"Do we have to put on ugly green clothes?" Zoey asked.

"No, Zoey, Honey, we are going to get something to eat," I said, as we began making our way to the structure which looked to be abandoned. Two outside lights were on, but I did not see any vehicles or people anywhere. It was quite dark in the surrounding area, but I was pretty sure there was no one around here. The building looked very dark, but only had a couple of windows, so the inside could be well-lit, and we wouldn't be able to see the light from where we were.

"My legs are getting tired," Mickey said. "I am not trying to complain, Daddy, but my legs ARE getting tired."

"My legs are tired too," Zoey said.

"We are almost there, and you can sit down when we get inside," he promised.

When we finally made it to the building, I felt a great sense of relief. Michael held the door open for us, but the girls stopped in their tracks.

"Daddy, it is really dark inside," Mickey said. "I'm scared."

"I don't wanna go in there," Zoey cried, clinging to me. "That is the darkest place I have ever seen in my whole life."

"I will go first, and I will find a light switch," I said, using the sound of my own voice to make me bold. It did look kind of scary inside since it was completely dark.

The girls scrambled to get behind me. We went through a little entryway and through a glass door. As I stepped into the room, the lights came on, scaring me.

"Who's there?" I asked, then I laughed when I realized the lights were activated by motion. "Is anyone here?" I called.

We had come into a small waiting room and the girls scrambled to sit on the chairs at one side of the room. Ahead of us was a glassed-in reception area. I hobbled over to lean on the counter. To our right was a steel door. Michael rushed to the door and pushed on it, but it was locked.

"What are we going to do now, Daddy?" Mickey asked, her eyes wide with concern. It occurred to me that a child so young should not have to worry about anything, much less be in a situation such as this one.

"Just a second, I am thinking," he said, examining the door for some way to open it.

I looked into the reception area to see if I could spot some food or a key, but I didn't see anything that could help us.

"Well, at least we can sleep in here tonight," I said, "and then we can figure out what to do tomorrow, after we have had some rest. Maybe someone will come here in the morning."

"Wait!" Michael said. "This door does not have a lock on it. It must open by a sensor."

Something hanging on the wall behind the reception desk caught my eye.

"The ID badge!" I said, pointing. "Right there! It must be a key!"

"How can we reach it?" Michael asked. His eyes lit up. "Maybe I can find some wire outside and make a hook."

I looked at the small opening in the glass, where items would be passed to and from the receptionist. "I have an idea. Zoey, come here."

"What do you want, Mommy?" Zoey asked, as she came over to me.

"She can fit through here!" I said. "Michael, can you lift her up? She is small enough to fit!"

"That might work!" Michael agreed.

"It WILL work!" I said. "Zoey, I want you to go inside here and get that card that is hanging on the wall. Can you do that for me?"

"Yes, Mommy, I can do that!" she said enthusiastically.

He picked her up and she scooted through the small opening and dropped onto the floor.

"It's right over there," I said.

"I can't reach it!" she said, jumping up to try to get it. Her little fingers were just short of being able to touch it.

"Maybe you can stand on something," I suggested. "Do you see anything you can stand on?"

"How about the chair?" she asked.

"Does it have wheels on it?" I asked. I could imagine what would happen if she were to fall, and I would be right here, so close, and not able to get to her.

"Yes, so I can move it," she said, as she began to roll it close to the wall.

"Wait!" Michael said, before she could climb up on it. She stopped and looked at him. "Find something to put by the wheels so they won't roll," he instructed.

"Like what?" she asked.

I couldn't see anything from where I was. That desk was spotless.

"Look inside the drawers," Michael told her.

She opened a drawer on the desk and began shuffling through items. "Like what?" she asked again. "A stapler? A pen? Note pads? A candy bar?"

"A candy bar?" Mickey said. "Can I have it?"

"You girls can share it," I said, as Zoey took the candy bar out of the drawer. "Let's check it first. We have no idea how old it is."

"I don't care how old it is!" Mickey said. "I am SO hungry!"

"Zoey, what else do you see?" Michael asked.

"A bunch of paper clips and those big clipper things," she said. "Some of the white tape stuff Mommy uses when she makes mistakes writing."

"Look in another drawer," I said. "There must be something."

"See if you can find any big erasers," Michael said.

She opened another drawer. "Here is a whole pack of them!" she said, holding it up to show us.

"Good! That's good!" Michael said. He told her where to place them so the chair would not move when she climbed on it. I was thankful for his engineer's mind. I had no doubt that his instructions would be perfect for this job.

After she had carefully placed the erasers around the wheels, she looked at Michael for confirmation.

"Okay, go ahead and climb up on the chair," he said, "but move slowly. Be very careful."

"I am always very careful," she told him.

While watching Zoey perform this task, I held my breath, as if breathing would somehow increase the risk of failure. She was a champion, moving slowly, standing carefully on the chair, grabbing the chain with the ID badge, and sitting down on the chair until her feet safely reached the floor again. I let out a sigh of relief as she handed the badge to me through the same opening she had gone through.

"Good girl!" Michael said.

I handed the badge to him and in about one step, he was back at the steel door.

"It works!" he said, as the latch released and the door opened on its own.

Mickey jumped up from the chair and began clapping her hands. "Let's go find some food!" she shouted.

"Mommy, how can I get out?" Zoey asked, as she struggled unsuccessfully to climb back up to the opening.

"That door!" I said, pointing to a door nearly camouflaged in the wall behind her. "You go through there, and we will meet you on the other side."

She opened the door, and as she stepped through it, I could see a light turn on in the room where she was going. The door closed behind her with a loud click.

"Zoey!" I yelled, trying unsuccessfully to get my head through the small window in the glass where she had entered.

I stood up and hurried (as fast as I could with my sore ankle) over to where Michael was holding the steel door, and the three of us went through it. A light came on, revealing that we were in a long hallway.

"Zoey? I asked. She was not in the same room as we were! "Zoey! I called. She had to be behind the wall to our left.

"Look, Daddy!" Mickey yelled excitedly. "It says 'kitchen' right over there!" She pulled her dad towards the kitchen.

"I have to get Zoey," I said, refusing to go any farther without my daughter.

"Here is the key card," Michael said, handing it to me, as he was being pulled toward the kitchen. "We will go to the kitchen and see if we can find any food while you go find Zoey. We will be right there waiting for you. I will even fix you dinner!"

I was very hungry, too, but I had to find Zoey. I was a little upset that Michael would choose to leave me, but I knew he had to take care of his own daughter, and now that we knew the way to the kitchen, all I had to do was find Zoey, and we would be able to get to the kitchen and eat.

The room Zoey had entered was on the left side of me. I hobbled over to a door to my left that was locked, so I waved the key card in front of the sensor and the door slowly opened.

"Zoey?" I called. I stepped into another long hallway, and the lights came on. "Zoey?"

Where was she? I was beginning to panic. No, no, no, this could not be happening! Where had happened to my daughter?

"Zoey!" I yelled at the top of my lungs.

Should I go down this hallway? Should I go back? Where was my daughter?

AN ANGEL APPEARS

Terry blinked against the bright light of the area he had entered. His eyes had become accustomed to the dark during the recent days, nights, weeks, however long it had been. He found himself inside a lounge area, with couches, chairs and tables, and several large screens mounted on the walls, but no people.

"Hello!" he called. "Is anyone here?"

He looked around for food or a vending machine, but he didn't see an edible item. It looked to him like this place hadn't been used in years. He crossed over to the steel door on the opposite side of the room, but it was locked. His shoulders sagged. He pounded on the door. He was still trapped; but at least now he had light and more room to move around.

"God," he said aloud, "I know You have not brought me all this way to leave me here to die," he said, making himself believe his own words. He spotted a drinking fountain, dashed over to it, and was so thankful it was working. "Rivers of living water," he mumbled, as he gulped it up.

His body was so happy to be out of the small, confined room he began jogging around this room as he tried to formulate a plan. What could he do? He had no phone, no means of communicating with anyone, no way to open the door, and nobody else here with him. But he was alive, he had hope. God must still have a purpose for his life, because he was still here.

He could not allow himself to focus on what he did not have. That was negative thinking. So, what did he have? He had his mind, the mind of an engineer, and he could use it to put something together to get out of here. He also had an abundance of furniture, which could not break open a steel door, but perhaps he could take apart of one of the chairs or tables to use to pick the lock. Yes, yes, that was a plan. He would be able to get out of here!

"Thank You, Lord!" he shouted, before he even had it figured out. He ran around the room a couple more times, at a much faster pace, feeling so good to finally be moving.

A loud click stopped him in his tracks. He looked expectantly at the steel door, as it slowly opened.

"Hi, Daddy," his daughter said, stepping through the door.

He leaped across the room in three giant steps, both to grab his daughter and to block the door from closing and locking them inside.

"Zoey!" he shouted, his foot against the door. He swooped her up and they left the room with her in his arms.

CAN THIS REALLY BE HAPPENING?

I limped down the hall as quickly as I could, using the key card on every door I approached. The first one did not open, and I was sure it led to the little reception area where Zoey had been, so I moved to the next door. The latch released, and the door opened slowly.

"Zoey!" I called into the dark room. "Zoey, are you in there? If you can hear my voice, answer me!"

I waited a moment, and she did not answer my call, so I let the door go closed and I moved to the next one. My heart was beating so hard, I was shaking, my head started pounding, and I felt tears escaping from my eyes. I had to be in a nightmare! Okay, it was time to awaken! The alarm would sound, and I would find myself at home, in my bed, sweating out a nightmare. This could not be happening to us! Wake up! Please, God, let me wake up!

"Dear God," I began to pray, through my tears, "I am asking You, please, I am begging You, let me find my daughter! She is Your daughter, too, please, she must be so scared! Help us to find each other in this... this place! You know where she is, so please, show me where she is! In the name of Jesus, I pray. Amen."

Saying the prayer did not bring my daughter instantly to me, but it did help me to calm down and to realize that, no matter how crazy this day had been, and no matter what was happening now, God was in control. He knew where Zoey was, right at that moment. He would not let anything happen to her.

I stopped and took a couple of deep breaths, then I hobbled down the hall to the next door. As I held up the key card, I heard the latch release. I knew Zoey had to be on the other side of this door.

The door slowly opened and I found myself looking into the kitchen.

"Oh, there you are!" Michael said, stepping around a large shelf. "I was starting to get worried about you. Did you find Zoey?"

"Look at all the food they have in here!" Mickey said, holding a large bag of potato chips under her arm and a couple of trays filled with all kinds of food. "I am fixing a tray for Zoey. Where is she?"

"I haven't found her yet," I confessed. "I looked in a few rooms, but she wasn't in any of them. The key doesn't work on all the doors."

"She has to be here," Michael assured me. "She can't be too far away. We are going to find her. You look like you are shaking. Maybe you should have something to eat, and then we can all go together and look for her."

"No, I can't stop looking for her," I said, too upset to eat. "I have to go and find her."

"Take a bite of this banana," Mickey said, holding it out to me. "You can think better after you eat a banana. That is what Daddy always tells me."

The banana did look very inviting, and my stomach started growling when I thought about eating it. "Okay, just this one banana, for energy, and then I need to go and look for her. Actually, I can take it with me."

I peeled the banana and had to force myself to not eat it all in one bite. I realized I hadn't eaten anything since this morning, because Karen had interrupted us before we had our lunch. Oh, poor Zoey must be so hungry by now, and so scared and alone, not knowing where I was.

"Someone must have been here recently," Michael observed, "because these bananas are still fresh."

"And there is milk in here!" Mickey said, holding the refrigerator door open. "There is a lot more food in here! We can have a feast!" She stopped and closed the refrigerator door. "Daddy, do we have to pay for all this food?"

Michael looked at me before answering. "When we find out who this food belongs to, we will pay for everything we eat," he promised.

"So, we can eat whatever we want, as much as we want?" Mickey asked. "Because we are going to pay for it," she added.

"We don't want to be greedy," Michael warned her. "And you don't want to get a stomach ache, either."

"Let's all go look for Zoey, and then we can have a feast together," she said, after a moment of thought. "It would not be not fair for us to eat whatever we want, when Zoey is lost and hungry somewhere in this place."

She stated my thoughts exactly.

THE LAST PLACE TO LOOK

Mickey and Michael put the mound of food they had collected onto one of the kitchen counters and we set off to find Zoey. As soon as we stepped into the long hallway, the lights came on so we could see a multitude of doors going all the way to the end of the hall.

"We should probably stay together, since we have only one key card," Michael said.

"And we don't want to get lost from each other," Mickey added.

"And I can't move very fast, so please be patient with me," I said. The pain in my ankle was great, but my need to find Zoey was greater.

"Here, you take the key," I said, handing it to Michael. "You can go a lot faster than I can."

The next three doors were locked, but the fourth one opened. The room was dark. The three of us stepped into the room and the lights turned on, revealing a large room with couches and large screens on the walls. Closed doors were on one side and the far end of the room. Mickey started to run around the room, stopping at each door and knocking, calling for Zoey.

"Zoey! Are you in here?" I called.

She did not reply.

"Should we go through here, and check those doors on the other side of this room, or should we check the next room down the hall?" Michael asked. "Is your mother's intuition telling you anything?"

"I know she is so close, but I don't know where!" I cried.

"I heard someone behind this door!" Mickey said. "Zoey, is

that you?" She pressed her ear against the door and listened.

Michael ran to her with the key, and I hopped over behind him.

When he opened the door, I was shocked to see a woman lying on the floor, whimpering. I was disappointed we had not found Zoey, yet glad we could help someone else.

"Lady, are you okay?" Mickey asked, as Michael rushed to her side.

"Let me help you," he said. "Are you hurt?"

She began to sob uncontrollably. Her clothes were dirty and torn, and she gripped a small blanket tightly. She was wearing a blue dress, not the fashion color of the day.

"It's okay, everything is going to be okay," I said, trying to sooth her. "We are going to get you out of here."

Her sobbing began to subside as she looked at me. "Where am I?" she whispered.

"This is the old prison," Michael said, "but it's closed down. We are going to get you out of here."

"Did the President send you?" she asked, her eyes darting back and forth from Michael to me.

"The President?" I said. "No, we were left here by some teenagers." I didn't want to go into the whole unbelievable story. "Come on, are you hungry? We found the kitchen, and there's all kinds of food there."

"Yes, thirsty," she said quietly. "I'm not sure what happened, or how I got here," she said. "The President kidnapped me and then he drugged me. I don't know what he did to me. I woke up and I was here."

"Well, let's get you something to drink and eat, and then we'll get out of here," Michael said, helping her to her feet. She was wobbly, but she leaned on Michael as he guided her out of her little room.

"Take her to the kitchen so she can get something to eat and drink," I said. "I need to find Zoey."

141

Mickey's eyes grew wide. "Do the lights go on automatically when we come in a room?" she asked.

"That's it!" I shouted. "She is in a room where the lights are on! The lights are activated by motion!"

"We could go down the hall and look under all the doors," Michael suggested, "and see if we can see any light shining anywhere."

"I could run down the hall and call her name," Mickey offered.

"Wait a minute," I said. "She doesn't have a key, so she can only go through doors that are not locked."

"Or she is still in the room on the other side of the office, you know, the first door she opened?" Michael said.

"I tried to find that room, but the key card didn't unlock it. This place is so big, and it's such a maze!" I said, feeling frustrated.

"She is in here, and we will find her," Michael promised.

The nearby couch was so inviting, I wanted to sit down and rest; but I could not stop until we found Zoey.

"Let's go back to the hall," I said, turning back to the door we had entered. "Mickey, you do what you said. Run down the hall and call Zoey. If she can hear you, she will answer. Michael, you and I can follow behind and try to look under the doors for any room where the light is on."

"Let me check those two doors first," Mickey said, running across the room. "Zoey! Zoey! Are you in there? Zooooeeeeey!" She tested the doors, and she bent down to look underneath them, to see if a light was on. Both doors were locked. "No light. She's not in these two rooms. Let's go find her!" she said enthusiastically, boosting my hope.

We returned to the long hall and Mickey immediately began running from door to door, calling for Zoey. Michael followed behind her, looking for a light and listening for a response, while the lady and I waited, leaning on each other for support.

"My name is Julia," she said softly.

I was about to respond when Mickey reached the end of the hall and turned back to us and shrugged.

"ZOOOOOEEEEY!!!!!!" I called, as loud as I possibly could. "WHERE ARE YOU?"

We waited for Zoey to answer, but we didn't hear a thing.

"Zoey is my daughter, and she got separated from us," I explained to Julia.

"We have to think this through," Michael said, returning to where we were standing. "They must have some kind of communication system, radios or intercoms or something," he said.

"We have looked everywhere we could," I said, holding back my panic. "Where can she be?"

"She is here, she is close," Michael said. "We are going to find her," he said with confidence. "Let's go back to the kitchen and get a bite to eat, then we will look again, the three of us, in every room this key will open."

"She could be trapped somewhere," I said, "and I know she is scared to be all alone in here."

Mickey ran back down the hall to join us. "Don't make yourself worry too much," she said. "We are going to find her."

My stomach was in knots. I didn't know how I was going to be able to eat a thing, but I could at least sit down for a minute while they ate; then we would find Zoey!

Mickey ran ahead of Michael and Julia and me, and I knew she was extremely hungry. She stopped at the door, staring at it, waiting for her father to bring the key. As he approached the door, she turned to us with a big smile on her face. She pointed to the bottom of the door.

I hurried as fast as I could as Michael used the key card to open the door, and Mickey jumped up and down.

"The light is on!" she shouted.

"That's because we were in there a few minutes ago…" I began, then stopped short, amazed beyond belief, as I looked through the open door. There, in the kitchen, standing at the counter and eating, were Zoey and Terry!

"Hi, Mommy!" Zoey said, giving me an enormous grin, with her mouth full of something that looked delicious.

A LONG WALK HOME

After a filling meal and good night's sleep on couches in a lounge, we decided to walk back to town. I could hardly believe Terry's story; well, I did believe it, because I knew he was telling the truth, but the story itself was unbelievable. He had been brought here the day he was taken from the parking lot at Zoey's school, and for a while, he had been treated like a prisoner in solitary confinement, but he had never been placed under arrest. Then, one day, the guards stopped coming to his door, and he had been left alone in this place, without explanation and without any food. Miraculously, last night, he discovered that the door to his cell was unlocked, so he went in search for something to eat. Then Zoey walked into the room where he was!

Julia told us her equally unbelievable story about how she had been at a company picnic and the new President of our country had started a conversation with her that eventually led to him forcing her into the presidential limousine and then drugging her and having his way with her. She had no recollection of being left here, and she was unsure of how long she had been here.

Michael and I shared our story of the teenagers who had brought us here, skipping over most of the wild details. I wanted to put it behind us and move ahead with our lives. I could fill in the particulars with Terry later.

Terry and Michael checked the premises (they didn't find anyone else) and found no vehicles available, so our only option was to start walking. We found several backpacks, and we loaded them with food and water for our hike. My ankle was feeling a bit better, but I knew I would not be able to walk fast or far. After searching for other items, we might need, such as flashlights (Terry found some), matches (we didn't find any), a first aid kit (I found one) and blankets (we found some), Michael came around a corner with a real life-saver: a heavy-duty wheel chair. Terry wrapped my ankle with materials he took out of the first aid kit.

"You can ride in this, and we can also load it up with another backpack of supplies," he said.

I was so relieved, until I realized someone was going to have to push me all the way home.

"We will take turns pushing," Terry said, reading my mind. "And if you feel like walking, you can do that, too."

We headed out early in the morning, just after the sun rose, and began on our trek back to civilization – or something that at one time had resembled civilization. I walked a very short distance at the beginning, all the way down the dirt road to the highway, but by the time we started on the highway, I had to get off my ankle. The girls were real troopers. They walked and skipped and played games as we plugged along on the deserted road. We walked for about an hour, then Michael suggested we take a short break to drink some water. We started going again and after a couple of hours, we found a grassy area off the road to stop and have a little snack. The girls spread the blankets and we sat on the ground, as if we were simply having a picnic.

"Guess what, Daddy," Zoey said. "I don't have to go to school anymore."

"Why do you say that?" Terry asked.

"Because it's true," she said. "They won't let me go any more, so Mommy is going to teach me everything I need to know."

Terry looked at me, and I nodded. This was not a good time to explain it.

"Daddy, can I stop going to school, too?" Mickey asked. "Zoey's mom can teach me, too!"

"We will have to talk about this later," Michael said.

"But I don't like it when everyone always makes fun of my clothes!" she said. "I don't want to wear ugly green clothes like everybody else!"

"I don't either," Zoey agreed. "I am glad I don't have to see those meanies anymore."

Just then, we heard the sound of a car approaching, the first one that had come down the road all day. Terry jumped up in an attempt to flag it down, but the car zipped passed without even slowing.

"It will have to be a bigger car than that one," I said, "to fit all six of us."

"If they can take one or two, we could come back with a car and get the rest," Michael said.

"No! I don't want to be away from Daddy anymore!" Zoey cried. "Or Mommy!"

"We should make a plan, just in case."

"You are the only one with a car, Michael," I said.

Terry looked at me sharply and raised an eyebrow.

"Among all the other bizarre things that have happened since you've been gone, your car was towed away and mine was in an accident," I said, not wanting to go into all the details at the time.

"Is that how you hurt your leg?" Terry asked.

"No, that was from when she jumped over the fence," Mickey answered for me.

"You jumped over a fence?" Terry asked, astonished.

"We could be here all day while I go through the entire story," I said, "but I am hoping we can get home today."

"Yes, let's get going," Terry agreed. "Come on, let's get all of our garbage picked up and put it in this sack. Then we can throw it away when we see a trashcan. Girls, you pick up the blankets." He helped me to my feet and I pushed the wheelchair over to the road and we all started walking. I was using the wheelchair for assistance. We had only gone a short distance when a familiar-looking van came up behind us and pulled over.

I looked over at Michael, afraid these were the same young

boys who had taken us to the prison. What would stop them from taking us back there?

Several young people jumped out of the van, three boys and two girls who were probably in their late teens. They walked up to us, looking us over.

"Well, what do we have here?" one young man asked.

Terry and Michael blocked the girls and me defensively.

"We are just walking down the road," Terry said.

"Yeah, that is what it looks like," one of the boys said.

"What do you think you are wearing?" the shorter girl asked. All five of them were dressed in the style of the day, 'ugly green,' as our daughters described it.

"We are wearing clothes we like," Zoey announced boldly. "I like pink and purple."

"You people are obviously not members of our society," the taller girl said. "You are wearing those old clothes, and I can tell you are doing something you do not want to do. Now, I am telling you this very calmly and with much respect, if you were one of us, you would have total freedom to do whatever you want. You people are slaves to the old system. Just look at you!"

"If I were you, I would take a look at you," Terry said. "Why are you dressed like that, all in the same color?"

"Man, it's cool," one of the boys said. "Don't you know anything?"

"Yeah, this is the way everyone is dressing," the shorter girl said, sticking out her chin at us.

"Everyone who is anyone dresses like this," the taller girl said.

"So, you call this freedom?" Terry asked. "What would happen if you were to wear another color, say, pink or purple?"

"Then we would be rejects from society, like you!" the tall girl said.

"And you call this freedom?" Michael asked. "You have to do

exactly what everyone else is doing. How is that freedom?"

The young people exchanged glances and took off for the van. They sped away so fast, we didn't have a chance to say goodbye.

The Unraveling of Society

The Order of the Day

"Mother, I am speaking to you in a very calm manner, and with much respect, and I am asking you to buy for me a new outfit. The ones I have are not the latest Vinnie Pinchey. Look at me! I am so ashamed! I can't go anywhere in these clothes, and let myself be seen out in public with last month's fashions."

"Janie, I am answering you in a very calm manner, and with much respect. I don't feel like going shopping right now, or any time today or tomorrow or the next day, because I have other things I want to do. Besides, you don't have any place to go until next week. You do not have one Vinnie Pinchey event scheduled this week, so you don't need anything right now."

"But mother, I really need some new clothes today. You don't have to go anywhere. You can get them online. I never said you had to go somewhere to buy clothes for me."

"Darling, you know you are larger than the regular Vinnie Pinchey size, so you can't buy your clothes online. You need to go to one of the Vinnie Pinchey stores that has larger sizes available and try them on. Or better yet, wait until your weight gets down, and then we will be able to buy your outfits online."

"I am not asking you to buy them online, Mother. Just give me your credit number and I will use my device to buy them."

"I am not giving you my credit number. You have to wait."

"But I don't want to wait! I want new clothes today! Or if I can't get them today, I want to order them today!"

"Too bad. This time what you want and what I want are in conflict, and because I am older, and I am your mother, I get what I want this time."

"But if I don't get what I want, that is not Vinnie Pinchey! Are you saying that you are denying me Vinnie Pinchey? You can't do that!" She stomped her foot defiantly.

"What I am saying is this: my Vinnie Pinchey trumps your Vinnie Pinchey this time."

In the Home

"Mother, why do we not have any clean dishes in this house?" Darlene yelled, loud enough for her mother to hear from the other room. Dirty dishes were stacked all over the counter and both sides of the sink were filled with them.

"Do you feel like washing them?" her mother called back. "I certainly do not feel like washing dishes – not ever. I have a lot of other things I want to do, and that does not leave me any time to do things I don't want to do."

"Hey, can you both stop yelling?" Darrell yelled from the living room. "I am trying to watch my program! This is something I really want to do! You have to respect that, even if you don't like it!"

"Mother, if you are not going to fix anything for us to eat, you could at least wash the dishes so I can make something for myself!" Darlene was very upset with her parents. After all, she had decided she wanted to help her dad when he and her mom were out in the back yard all day, and by doing that, she had practically saved his life. Her parents should be more grateful to her, and they should want to do things for her instead of only for themselves.

Well, it really did not matter what they did or didn't do, since she was going to do whatever she wanted to do, and she was not going to do anything she did not want to do. She did not want to wash any dishes, so she would have to eat something right out of the carton. She was looking forward to the day when she could move out of this house and live on her own. In fact, she wanted to move out right away. She would start making plans today. This whole family thing wasn't like it used to be. They never did anything together as a family, and they didn't even act like they liked each other anymore. What was the importance of a family, if her mother and father no longer did anything for her, or bought her what she wanted?

Today, this very afternoon, she would gather her things together and prepare to move out of this sorry house that could no longer be called a home.

At the Auto Shop

"Mack! Is my car ready yet?" Nick called, as he looked around the shop for his vehicle.

"Oh, no, Nick, I haven't started working on it yet."

"But I left it here a week ago, and all it needs is one little adjustment. You said it would only take about an hour to fix it."

"Yes, that is true. I did say that. And it will only take about an hour to fix it, as soon as I get started on it."

"You haven't even started on it yet?"

"Ahhh, Nick, you catch on fast. I am telling you in the most calm and respectful manner, I have not started working on it yet."

"Well, why not? You have had it here for a whole week! I need my car!"

"I want to work on my own car. Look at this baby. Isn't she sweet? I have been restoring her for the last two months, and since I haven't had any interruptions, I have been able to get a lot done on her. Isn't she nice-looking? If I didn't have so much time to work on her, I probably would never be able to get her done!"

"But I need you to fix my car! Come on, it will only take you one hour! You said so yourself."

"I don't feel like working on it now. When I feel like taking a break from working on my own project, then I will work on your car. By the way, I have to say, all this walking you have been doing lately is beginning to give you a nice physique."

"Come on, Mack! Can't you do my car right now? I really need it to get across town to the woods, so I can get to my next level. It is way too far to walk, and we never know when the buses are going to be running any more, if I would stoop low enough to ride a bus. Come on. I need my car. Time is not standing still. I will wait. You said it will only take an hour to make the adjustments. I have an hour right now, if you do."

"No can do, my friend. I am telling you in a calm and respectful manner, in this case, at this time, my Vinnie Pinchey wins. Come back tomorrow. Who knows? Maybe I'll feel like working on it then. You never can tell."

AT THE STORE

"Excuse me! Excuse me!" Carmen looked around the store, but couldn't find anybody working there. She needed to buy something for her headache, but the shelves that usually had pain relievers were completely bare.

"Is anybody working here today?" she called out.

A young man came sauntering down the aisle toward her. "Do you need something, Miss?"

"Yes, I need something for my headache. I don't see anything on any of the shelves."

"Have you been eating enough rutabagas lately, Miss?"

"Of course, I have been eating enough rutabagas! I just need something for my headache."

"You know, it is not Vinnie Pinchey to have a headache. So, why would we have anything on the shelf for headache?"

"Because my head hurts!"

"Did you already go to your doctor?"

"I tried to go to the doctor, but I couldn't make an appointment because the receptionist was all Vinnie Pinchey, and she didn't feel like making an appointment for me."

"Well, there's not really anything I can do for you here. The young man who stocks these shelves is also all Vinnie Pinchey, and he doesn't feel like working right now."

"Do you have any idea when he will feel like working again?"

"Do I have any idea when he will feel like working again? Ha-ha-ha! You are so funny. You should be a comedian. Is that what you would like to do? If that is what you want to do, go ahead and do it! Go all Vinnie Pinchey!"

"I am not trying to be funny!" she said angrily. "I am asking you in a calm and respectful manner, when can I expect for the shelves to be stocked again? Or can you go in the back room and find a bottle of pain relievers for me, for my headache?"

"Well, now, you are crossing the line, Miss. Are you trying to tell me what to do? You can't tell me what to do."

"Yes, indeed, I am trying to tell you what to do. I am asking in a calm and respectful manner; can somebody bring me any kind of a pain reliever? Or can I go in the back and get one myself?"

"Well, Miss, I cannot tell you what you can or cannot do. But I will give you a clue. Hey, I made a rhyme and I wasn't even trying! Maybe I should be a poet! Ha-ha-ha!"

"So, you are saying it is okay for me to go in the back room and find my own pain reliever?"

"If that is what you really want to do. Or, I should say, if you want to waste your time, go ahead, the door is right over there."

"Why do you say I would be wasting my time? I really need a pain reliever, and may I say, you are not helping my headache one bit."

"You may say that. And I am saying you would be wasting your time because you would be wasting your time. The man who makes our deliveries doesn't feel like driving anymore, so we haven't had a delivery in about three weeks. It is so amazing how quickly the shelves go bare if you don't restock them, even when most of the people don't feel like shopping so are not coming to the store these days."

"Well, thank you for your non-help," she said rubbing her head with both hands, pressing her head between them. "I am going to have to find another store. I really need a pain reliever, right now."

"Good luck in finding another store that's open around here. Most people don't feel like going to work anymore. In the best Vinnie Pinchey fashion, they don't have to go to work. They are doing whatever they want to do."

"So, why are you still here? Why are you not doing whatever

you want to do?"

"I like to work here. I especially like it with all the other employees gone, and now that I don't have to do any real work. I show up here, and somehow, I am still getting a paycheck, and that is good enough for me. Then I can buy all the Vinnie Pinchey accessories I want."

"This is what you want to do? How does this help your customers?"

"Hey, I have a better idea! If you want to get rid of your headache, follow me."

She followed him through aisles and aisles of empty shelves until they finally arrived at some shelves that were overflowing with items – two different items, to be exact.

"Here we are!" he announced gleefully, presenting the shelves with an outstretched hand.

"What is this?" she asked, although she actually knew what these items were.

"Well, Miss, here you have it! One of these will certainly take away your headache! Or you could pamper yourself and try both, if I may say so myself, no offense intended. Over here we have your Vinnie Pinchey nutritional shakes, in a variety of all your favorite flavors, including rutabaga, and over on this side, we have your Vinnie Pinchey supplements!"

"But I have a headache now!" she cried.

"And if you would indulge yourself, or treat yourself, or, should I say, if you would take care of yourself and your nutritional requirements by the intake of these two products, I can guarantee you, you will never again have a headache. I am telling you in a calm and respectful manner, you should have been stocking up and partaking of these two items all along, until now, and then, now, you would not be here, right here, right now, in this very store, complaining to me about having a headache. So, there you have it! How many of each item would you like? If you start taking both of these products today, I will never see you here again, crying that you have a headache."

"Is this all you have in this store?" she asked, squeezing her head with both hands, in an effort to relieve the pounding pain.

"What else could you possibly need from a store like this? You can get all the rutabagas you need at the grocery store. We don't carry them here. I guess you already know that, though, don't you? Oh, that look is not good on you, Miss. Please, I must ask you in a calm and respectful manner, please remove your hands from your head. Yuk!"

"My head is killing me!" she shouted at him. "I need a pain reliever, and I need it right now!"

"My, my, are we so not Vinnie Pinchey!" he said, taking a step away from her. "These are the two options we have for you, Miss, take it or leave it. And you need to make your decision right now, because I do not feel like serving you any longer. I want to go sit down now, and I will do just that, right now, unless you are planning to purchase an item."

"I don't want to buy any Vinnie Pinchey nutritional shakes or Vinnie Pinchey diet pills! I want to buy a pain reliever, to get rid of my splitting headache!"

"Well, then, I can't help you with that one. You are on your own."

"You are right about one thing," she called after him, as he walked away from her. "You will not see me here again!"

She left the store with her headache in full force. How could she get any help, when everyone around here was all Vinnie Pinchey?

On the Job

Nick wandered toward the office where he was to meet his boss. He was a few minutes late, well, forty-two minutes late, to be exact, but he did not really want to be here. His boss was probably going to thank him for doing something he really did not want to do, like showing up to work.

"Hey, Izzy!" Nick said, reaching out to shake his hand as he entered the office. "What is new with you?"

"I could very well be asking you that very question, Nick," Izzy replied, not returning the handshake, but towering his fingertips with his elbows resting on the desk.

"Well, to tell the truth, things are going quite well," Nick said, "except for my car. I can't get it out of the shop because the guy is well, you know, he's all Vinnie Pinchey and he doesn't want to work it. He said he doesn't feel like it."

"What a coincidence," Izzy said. "He is not the only one who doesn't feel like working these days."

"Oh, you, too?" Nick asked, settling into a chair. "Yeah, I know how you feel, I mean, isn't it the way it is these days? Who feels like working, especially when we can do anything we want? Man, are these not the golden days? Who has ever had it better than we have it today? Everything we could possibly want, right in our hands, just like that!" He displayed his hands, to emphasize his point.

"Hey, did you know I finally made it to level five in round three? I bet you can never guess where that took me. I had to follow – on foot, mind you – I had to follow my clues and hints all the way to the park out by the river! And it was not easy, I am telling you, I mean, I had to walk the whole way, and then I had to wade into the stream, and then, get this! I had to climb a tree! Do you know how hard it is to climb a tree with one hand? I thought I was going to fall, and I almost dropped my device right into the river, but I was finally able to aim it right at the multiple hidden figures and obtain the treasure!"

"Well, that is what I want to talk to you about," Izzy said, as he folded his hands on his desk.

"Hey, sorry, Man, I can't give you any hints," Nick said, shaking his head. "Your challenge is completely different from my challenge. You know that. What can I say?"

"You are correct, Nick, my challenge is completely different from your challenge," he agreed, nodding his head as he looked at his hands.

"Well, yeah," Nick said. "How could we have an individual challenge, if all of ours are the same?" He smiled confidently at his supervisor.

"I am sorry to have to say it this way, Nick, but I am going to have to let you go."

"Let me go? Go where?" Nick asked, confused. "Oh, you mean to the next level? Oh, yeah, I've got that, Izzy! I am already there! I mean, I haven't actually started, but in here," he tapped the side of his head, "I've got it already figured out, how and where I am going to go next, in the next level."

"No, that is not what I am saying, Nick," Izzy said. "Listen to me. Listen carefully to my words I am saying in a calm and respectful manner. I am letting you go from your job, Nick. You have not been at work but one time in the last three weeks, and even that day, you didn't do any work."

Nick stared at Izzy with a look of incomprehension. He tilted his head sideways a bit and waited, still not understanding the meaning of his words.

"What are you saying, then?" he asked.

"Nick, I don't want to have to say this, but I have to say this. This is something I really don't want to do, and you know how hard it is these days to do something you don't want to do. It goes against every idea of today's society. Okay, here I go. This is what I have to say but I don't want to say: You are fired, Nick."

"If you don't want to say it, then why are you saying it?" Nick asked. "We don't have to do anything we don't want to do. That is the order of the day. Even our president of this great country told us we don't have to do anything we don't want to do. Didn't you hear his speech?"

"Of course, I heard his speech," Izzy said, "but just because he said it, that doesn't mean we can always do whatever we want all the time."

"Oh, yes it does!" Nick protested. "The president announced it, so we need to follow his orders!"

"It wasn't so much an order as it was a suggestion," Izzy replied.

"What are you talking about? Are you one of the rebels in disguise?" Nick asked loudly, hoping to get some support from anyone who may be listening.

"I am so sorry, Nick, but you no longer work here," Izzy said. "Your final paycheck will be deposited into your account."

"You are serious?" Nick asked, still unable to believe what he was hearing.

"Look at it this way, Nick," Izzy said with a smile. "I think this is actually something you want. Now you can spend all of your time working on your challenge. You don't even have to think about this job anymore."

At the Hospital

"I am sorry to have to say this to you, but this is not the time to come in with an emergency," Winnie said to the young couple who had brought their baby to the hospital emergency room.

"But our baby is really sick!" the girl said. Winnie thought she looked to be about fifteen years old.

"We can't do anything for your baby today," Winnie said. "None of our doctors wanted to come in today. The three nurses who wanted to work are too busy taking care of patients who are already here. Maybe it will be better if you want to bring her – is it a girl? She's all in pink – try bringing her back tomorrow. Maybe one of the doctors will want to come in then."

"We don't want to come back tomorrow!" the young man said. "Our baby is sick now!"

"As you well know, you don't have to do anything you don't want to do, so, then, don't come back tomorrow." Winnie smiled at them, proud that her logic made so much sense.

"She needs to be seen by a doctor today!" the young mother cried. "We want a doctor to look at her now!"

"Oh, that is a tough one," Winnie said apologetically. "This is one thing both of you obviously want, but we can't give it to you. Oh, please, don't look so sad. That is not anything near a Vinnie Pinchey face! Come on, give me a more pleasant look. I don't want to see you looking so sad. And since I don't want to see it, you either have to change your expression, or I must ask you to leave."

"But what about our baby?" the young man asked. "She is really sick, and we need someone to look at her now!"

"I absolutely did not want to be the one to tell you," Winnie said, lowering her voice, "but you two obviously were doing exactly what you wanted to do, a while back, and now you have a baby. Sometimes when we only do what we want to do, we are stuck with consequences, and we run out of options to deal with those consequences. See? Even I, without wanting it, had to do something I didn't want to do. I had to tell you this important fact, and I really did not want to do that. Now, you must do something you don't want to do. You must go home now. We can't help you. Go and do something else you want to do. I am sure you have plenty of other things you want to do."

The Way of the Rebellion Comes Home

"Mommy," Zoey said, in her sweetest little voice. I had a feeling she was going to ask me for something, and after all she had been through, I wanted to give her heart's desire, in an effort to try to ease the pain, take away some of the harsh memories she held in her young mind.

"Yes, Sweetie?" I asked. Although she was still only six years old, she had a look about her that said she was much wiser than a six-year-old. I was a bit wounded by her loss of innocence at such a young age. She should not have to worry about such things as had come upon our family in these few short months.

"Mommy, can I have a Vinnie Pinchey doll?"

Available from Everlasting Publishing

Novels by Dana Pride

- » *Vinnie Pinchey*
- » *Immediate Search*
- » *Hope Continually*
- » *The Hidden City*
- » *So How is THAT a Bully?*
- » *After the Great Devastation*
- » *The Red Cloak*
- » *Nightmares of Murder*
- » *No One Like You*
- » *Existing*
- » *All These Things*
- » *Kissing a Dead Man*

Non-fiction books by Dana Pride

- » *Perceptions of Perfection: 66 Poems for a Rock Star*
- » *How to Get Fat Without Even Trying*
- » *What Really Happened in Mexico*
- » *We Choose our Memories: Sayings of the Young Folks*
- » *We Choose our Memories: Sayings of the Old Folks*

Poetry books by Joseph Fram

- » *Joseph's Journey, Volume 1*
- » *Joseph's Journey, Volume 2*
- » *Joseph's Journey, Volume 3*
- » *Joseph's Journey, Volume 4*
- » *Joseph's Journey, Volume 5*
- » *Joseph's Journey, Volume 6*
- » *Joseph's Journey, Volume 7*
- » *Joseph's Journey, Volume 8*

Books by Steven Lowell-Martin

- » *Four Pounds of Pressure*
- » *Coptales*
- » *Moses' Chisel*

Full-color books

- » *Baby Bugs' Best Time, by Katelyn Spurlock*
- » *Nathan is Nathan, by Jahla*
- » *Nathan Art: Autistic-Artistic, by Nathan*

All titles also available as e-books

Everlasting Publishing
PO Box 1061
Yakima, Washington 98907
USA

http://everlastingpublishing.org